THE
OBSESSION

Published by Blue Dragon Publishing, LLC
Williamsburg, VA
www.BlueDragonPublishing.com
Copyright © 2016, 2018 by Dawn Brotherton

ISBN 978-1-939696-33-5 (Large Print)
ISBN 978-1-939696-80-9 (paperback)
ISBN 978-1-939696-15-1 (ePub)

Previously titled It's the Right Thing to Do
ISBN 978-0-9832454-0-7

Cover by Hakm Bin Ahmad

Printed in the U.S.A

27 26 25 24 23 22   4 5 6 7 8 9

THE
OBSESSION

Dawn Brotherton

DAWN BROTHERTON

Col, USAF, ret

Blue Dragon Publishing

Other books by Dawn Brotherton

Jackie Austin Mysteries

The Obsession

Wind the Clock

Truth Has No Agenda

Eastover Treasures

The Dragons of Silent Mountain

Untimely Love

SECTION I

MISSOURI, EARLY 1990S

Chapter 1

There was so much blood.

Police Officer Lieutenant Kyle Young entered the crime scene slowly, taking in everything as he went. Young was a well-built man in his early forties. His cropped, black hair was remnant of his days in the Army and so was his dedication to the job.

The small house was neat, making the spattering of blood all the more obscene. The windows in the living room were without curtains or shades, but that wasn't uncommon in this development. The nearest neighbors weren't close enough to look in from their homes, and the one-story house was set far enough from the road that a driver would have to stop to be able to catch a glimpse in the window.

The striped wallpaper appeared to be modern and newly applied. The furniture was inviting, but the matching throw pillows and blankets were scattered across the floor; their floral patterns obscured by a deep red bloodstain.

As Young made his way to the kitchen on his right, he followed two sets of bloody footprints—one barefoot and small, the other considerably larger with no tread. The phone was off the hook, and books were scattered around the room. Drawers were pulled out. Blood splattered the refrigerator, stove, and walls. The small table was off-kilter in the middle of the floor.

Young continued following the blood trail. Leading to the hallway were finger smears in red where someone had grabbed the door frame. In the hall off the kitchen lay the trim figure of a woman. She was face down in an unnatural position. Her light hair was now crimson. The walls were covered with blood spray dried to dark brown. A red pool that looked like a prop from a movie set had formed beneath her head.

"Has she been processed?" Young asked the technicians on the scene.

A tech rose from his position near the body. "We're done with her. We've bagged her hands in case, but her fingernails were pretty short. I don't know if we'll be able to get anything. Looks like she put up a fight though." He gathered his kit and followed his crew out of the room.

Another officer approached Young as he stood looking at the body. The clothes were slightly askew but still covered her. The metallic smell of blood was thick in the air.

"What do we know about her?" Young asked.

The officer consulted his notebook. "Miss Jane Albright, age twenty-six, a teacher at Warrensburg High School. Recently divorced. She bought this house about six months ago. We've just started canvassing the neighbors. So far, it sounds like she kept to herself although people have been seen coming and going on the weekends. Nothing extraordinary," he said. Gesturing to the stacks of wallpaper and carpet samples stacked against the wall, he added, "Look around at this house. She was probably trying to fix it up."

Young took a long look around the room, taking it all in. "When was the last time anyone saw her?"

"The guy in the next house oversaw her take the trash out when he was on his way home last night. She waved at him, but they didn't exchange any words. It was about eight."

"Who found her?" Young's gaze settled on the framed pictures propped against the wall—unfinished business that would never be finished now.

The officer flipped to the next page in his notebook. "The secretary from the school called her a few times this morning when she didn't show up for work. She never answered her phone, so the principal drove by on his way home. Apparently, he lives in the next neighborhood over. He saw the lights on and stopped. Looked through the front windows, saw the mess, and called the police."

Young looked around thoughtfully. "Guess it's too much to ask if you found the murder weapon lying around?"

"Nothing yet. She was stabbed with something, but that only accounts for some of her wounds. She was badly beaten before she died."

"Maybe they'll find trace on her." Young shook his head in disgust. "Not even safe in her own house," he muttered.

Chapter 2

Hello?" Silence. "Hello?" *This is getting old*, Jackie Austin thought as she replaced the phone and turned back to her latest project—mudding the sheetrock. This had to be her least favorite part of restoring this old house.

She stretched her back by reaching to the ceiling then bending to touch her toes. After a few more stretches, Jackie wiped her hands before tucking the brown, stray strands of hair behind her ears. Having played sports for many years, she was conditioned to a good workout, but putting up sheetrock, mudding, and taping required muscles previously undeveloped.

She caught her reflection in the cheap, full-length mirror she'd propped up against the wall of her bedroom. "Time to get back to the gym," she said to the silence. With a decent figure, Jackie always thought of herself as average looking, not as a head-turner. Her frame was slim, yet she lacked long, runway-model legs.

Jackie was quite happy with being average on the whole. She told herself she would prefer to be noticed for her brains or abilities, rather than her looks.

The phone rang again. Jackie glared at it, willing it to stop ringing. The constant phone calls with no one on the other end were driving her crazy. When she heard her mother's voice come over the answering machine, she grabbed the receiver.

"Hi, Mom."

"Hi, darling. How's it going?" It was always nice to hear from her mother. They didn't talk very often because Jackie's work schedule was so unpredictable.

"It's great. If only the mud fairy would come and finish these walls, I'd have it made."

Her mom quietly chuckled. "I'm still waiting for a little elf to clean my bathroom."

"Can't you get Alison to do it for you?"

"Are you suggesting your sister is an elf? She might not appreciate that."

"So what is my non-elfish sister up to in her spare time?"

"She's helping out at the library on the weekends. For some reason, your sister likes sorting the donated books for the book sales—says it soothes her."

"How many does she buy to take home with her?" Jackie knew her sister very well.

"Her bookshelves are overflowing."

That was one of the few ways the two sisters were alike. Although Alison was two years older, she was more of an introvert and had never moved away from their hometown. Jackie couldn't wait to get away.

She had joined the Air Force against her father's advice, selecting a career field that, until the late 1970s, was open only to men. The only female in her military training school, she had finished second in her class, but when she reported to Whiteman Air Force Base in Missouri, she had to demonstrate her worth to a whole new set of peers, instructors, and bosses.

But she loved taking on new challenges, and her latest project was tasking her in a whole new arena. Jackie's dad said she was a fool to buy a house. She was only twenty-three years old and didn't know the first thing about making such a large commitment, but Jackie believed she was making the right choice with this purchase.

Jackie had read the books, researched the points, and studied the interest rates; paying rent was like throwing money away. Now that she had a steady military paycheck, the timing to buy was perfect. And the fact that her dad said she couldn't do it was all the more reason to go ahead with her decision.

"Tell Alison she can bring me some books when she comes to see me. I'll read them at work," Jackie said.

"I don't understand how you can get any reading done at work," her mother said for the hundredth time. "Don't you have other things you should be doing?"

It was hard to explain her routine as a missile launch officer to someone outside the career field, let alone to someone outside the military. "Mom, we have to be underground twenty-four hours at a time. There's only so many times you can run the checklists. We're there just in case."

She didn't have to explain what she meant by *just in case*. Her mother knew that much. Jackie and her crew partner were prepared to respond in case of the catastrophic need to launch an intercontinental ballistic missile. Although they drilled constantly for that eventuality, Jackie didn't really believe it would ever come to that. The fact that crews all over the United States were sitting ready was enough of a deterrent for America's enemies.

"But, when I'm not underground, I have a lot of work to do around the house, so I'm going to let you go. I love you," Jackie said.

"I love you too," her mother replied. "Call us soon!"

"Yes, ma'am." Jackie hung up the phone and stood still for a minute, taking in the room.

As soon as she laid eyes on this house, she had fallen in love. It was the first one she'd looked at when she moved to Warrensburg, Missouri. The white, single-story house had a wraparound porch with ivy lovingly climbing up the trellis. The many windows and doors provided adequate circulation to cool the house as there was still no air conditioning. The kitchen even had a small, screened-in porch off the side of the house to allow for eating outside the warm house. The mother-in-law's apartment attached to the back could help with the mortgage when she got it fixed up and rented out. While a second lieutenant's pay was not measly, she could use all the extra income she could get.

Jackie had looked at numerous houses but kept coming back to the house with the ivy. Even the realtor had tried to talk her out of it because of the extensive work it needed, but Jackie would not be put off. She made an offer on the house, and it was accepted within a week. Because the house was owned by a woman who'd recently gone into a nursing home, the family threw in all the furniture, so they wouldn't have to move it.

While she knew she'd made the right decision, living alone had some disadvantages. At night the one-hundred-year-old house had its share of unnerving noises. Logically, Jackie knew it was the house settling, but logic didn't slow her pounding heart as she lay awake in bed . . . just listening.

Then the phone calls had started. It wasn't every night, but at least two or three times a week. The phone would ring, but when she answered, no one spoke on the other end.

It reminded Jackie of how she and Alison used to play tricks on their mother. Using the old rotary phones, the girls would dial their home phone number, quickly hang up and then hide, stifling giggles. The phone would ring back. Their mother would answer it, but no one was there. Several prank calls later, their mother would roust them from their hiding place and send them on their way.

It didn't seem as funny to Jackie now that it was happening to her. Even though phones had progressed to push buttons and the trick of dialing your own number didn't work anymore, Jackie still felt as though someone was hiding and laughing at her every time she answered the phone.

~

"Mae, is this a flower or a weed?" Jackie called to her friend sitting on the front porch.

"That one should stay, but the one next to it needs to be pulled. They'll quickly overrun your garden." Mae Wade leaned back on the porch steps as she oversaw Jackie's efforts.

Mae was an elderly woman who lived next door to Jackie in the quiet, family neighborhood. She had to be close to sixty-five, but Jackie wasn't about to ask her. She was in great shape and could often be found puttering around in her garden or mowing her grass. She wouldn't even think of letting anyone else do it. She was used to being independent and planned on staying that way.

"I don't know what I would do without you." Jackie tugged on the stubborn plant with one hand as she pushed the hair out of her face with the other.

"Oh, you'd manage fine . . . your garden might not though."

"Ha, ha." Jackie grinned from ear-to-ear.

"Ellie called on me yesterday." Mae referred to the neighborhood gossip living on the other side of Jackie's house. "Wanted to gab about the odd hours you keep."

Jackie had heard this before. Theirs was an older neighborhood, and the houses were close together. When Jackie, as a single woman, bought the McCall's place, it caused quite a stir around the small town. On top of that, the neighbors couldn't help but notice her schedule, coming and going at all hours and sometimes not bothering to come home at all. Because she had no garage or even a driveway, the absence of Jackie's little, black Taurus was easily noticed on many nights. It was enough to fuel the small-town gossip.

"And what did you tell them?"

Mae smiled as she watched Jackie struggle with a defiant weed. "Why the truth, of course! You spend your evenings with a variety of men—sometimes even overnight!"

Mae laughed out loud when Jackie's face snapped up to look at her.

"Mae, you're stirring up the neighbors!"

"It keeps my heart young."

Jackie's schedule as a missilier varied greatly from day-to-day and kept her neighbors guessing. She knew they liked to chatter, and her life gave them something to chat about, so she didn't mind. At least to them, her life seemed exciting.

She'd already explained the life of a missilier to Mae, who seemed to catch on better than Jackie's mother. The missile launch career field was comprised mainly of men—as were most fields in the Air Force. Jackie had a male crew partner. Every third night was spent on alert down in a capsule with another missilier overseeing ten Minuteman II Intercontinental Ballistic Missiles for twenty-four hours. On alternate days, she had various training to maintain proficiency.

"When do you have to work again?" Mae asked.

"I have alert tomorrow and Wednesday. Hopefully I'll be able to finish the front garden today and the living room walls when I get home. The realtor is going to hook me up with a handyman who might be able to fix the ceiling for me. He says they use him often, and he's reasonable."

"Keep attacking those weeds, and you'll be done in no time. Then I won't be able to tell you what to do anymore."

Chapter 3

The body seemed sadly cold and vulnerable on the autopsy table.

"Anything new on Miss Albright?" Young asked as he entered the morgue and spotted Tony Wright. Tony was a proper, tidy man of fifty-five. His signature polo shirt and khakis were hidden by the white lab coat he wore.

The chief medical examiner was engrossed in his work and didn't look up from the young lady on the table. "He didn't hit her with his fists. That doesn't give us much chance for DNA."

Young walked closer to the table, joining Wright. "What did he hit her with? She's pretty banged up."

Wright picked up a sharp scalpel to begin the next phase of the autopsy. "The damage to her face was blunt force—something with a corner but not your usual weapon. Look for some type of vase or heavy statue."

Young instantly had an idea what the weapon might have been. The crime scene investigators had found a vase made out of a green stone very popular in Korea and Japan. "I'll bring over what we found and have you look at it for comparison, but I'm fairly certain it was a celadon vase. The main body is rounded and heavy, but the base has an edge to it."

Wright nodded his head and continued, "That may explain the trauma to her head. The stab wounds to her abdomen are consistent with a kitchen knife like the others found in her house. Have they recovered the missing one yet?"

"Not yet but we're still searching the area. There are a lot of trees, and the houses are far apart. No one remembers seeing anything."

"They would have remembered seeing a man covered in blood."

Young made his way back to the squad room. Concordia was a small town of just over two thousand people. He knew nothing like this had happened in the last fifty years. He decided to dig deeper through the history files.

Some of the larger towns in Missouri had started to load their information into the new computer program the state had instituted. Concordia's funding only covered a half-dozen computers that the entire police station personnel—all twenty-four of them—shared. Since no one had authorized the funding for a data entry clerk, Young would have to go through the paper files, the way it had been done for years.

Chapter 4

It was after two on Monday afternoon when Jackie made it home from alert. The day was bright and breezy, and she was looking forward to getting out of her blue missile jumpsuit. She pulled up to her house, pleased to see that all the work she was doing in the garden was paying off. The purple and yellow flowers added color to the white backdrop of the house.

Parking in her usual spot alongside the curb, she got out and approached the house. When she stepped onto the front porch, she noticed that the front door was slightly ajar. *That's odd*, she thought.

With more curiosity than concern, she cautiously approached the house, pushing the door open. She stepped in, looking around. Nothing seemed out of place, although it was hard to tell with all the construction going on inside. She made her way around the piles of debris and slowly walked into her bedroom, straining her ears for any unusual sounds.

Nothing. Her TV was still in place as well as the VCR and her jewelry box. I must have left the door open when I went to work yesterday, Jackie chided herself. I need to be more careful.

The doorbell rang, and Jackie jumped. After taking a deep breath, she peered out the window that faced the front of the house. It was Keith Swanson, the handyman her realtor had shown her a picture of. Jackie went around to the front door, opening it for him. "Welcome to my humble abode," she announced with mock formality.

Keith smiled, shaking her hand. He was powerfully built with a broad chest and sandy hair. Jackie guessed he was in his early thirties.

"I think it's great that you're taking on this project alone. Not many women would do that," Keith said, looking around the room.

"Not many women are as stupid as I am," Jackie replied with a grin. "Come on in, and I'll show you around."

Jackie spent the next half-hour outlining the work she wanted Keith to accomplish. The ceiling in the living room needed to be sheetrocked and then sprayed with textured paint. The back bedroom that Jackie was going to use as an office needed a drop ceiling. The plaster ceiling was too bowed to keep, but Jackie didn't feel like going through the mess of tearing it out as she did in the front two rooms of the house.

She passed Keith a key. "I'll be at work all day tomorrow for training. Then Wednesday I leave for alert, so you'll have most that day and part of Thursday."

"I'll have it done by the time you get back on Thursday," he assured her.

"Good luck," she said.

∾

The operations group was housed in a plain, two-story, brick building. It reminded Jackie of a schoolhouse—nothing exceptional, walls lined with pictures of previous commanders from each of the squadrons.

Inside the office space set aside for the squadron, people were busy preparing for the day. Technical orders were checked, paperwork filed, and briefings prepared.

"Hey, Jackie."

Jackie turned to see the squadron adjutant coming down the hall. "Hi, Kris. What's going on?"

The captain gave the standard "who knows" shrug and leaned against the wall next to Jackie.

"Did you get any sleep last night?" Kris asked.

"A whole night without hang-ups," she said. "Can you believe it?" As one of Jackie's best friends, Kris Clark knew all about the problems she was having with the nuisance calls.

"I wish you would do something about them. Whoever is messing with you can't be normal."

"Probably just someone looking for attention," Jackie said, making light of it. "I don't want to give him the satisfaction of knowing it's getting to me."

Changing the subject, Kris asked, "Want to come over for dinner this weekend? Alex will grill chicken."

"You're going to go broke if you keep feeding me . . . but I'll be there. Can I bring anything?"

"Just you, unless you have a gorgeous hunk you want to drag along." Kris pushed herself away from the wall, heading back to her office. "I certainly wouldn't mind the view."

Smiling, Jackie continued to the squadron briefing room. She truly appreciated Kris. Jackie hadn't realized how much she needed female companionship until she spent four months of missile training at Vandenberg Air Force Base, California, surrounded by men. Many women would welcome that chance, but to Jackie it was uncomfortable.

In high school, she was always one of the guys. In college, boys started to notice her, but she was concentrating so much on getting through her classes (and working to pay for them) that she didn't have much time for dating. Since entering active duty, it was a whole different dynamic.

The men she met were all military, so at least they had that in common. At first, they were drawn to her outgoing personality. Once they realized she also had brains and was their competition for placement in class standings at Vandenberg and various awards and recognition within the squadron here at Whiteman, they looked at her differently.

She was someone to be wary of, even threatened by. Some still asked her out, but when she turned them down, even kindly, she was instantly labeled as the ice queen.

Jackie knew she was making good decisions though. She was breaking new ground as one of the first female missile launch officers on a co-ed crew, and she was sure to run into her share of troubles that would go along with that.

Soon after she arrived on base, she had gone to lunch with the Bravo Flight Commander, Mike Conklin. By the next day, the rumor mill was already in full motion. Mike thought it was funny, but the attention was unsettling for Jackie. She would much rather be the ice queen than the butt of so many jokes.

Jackie glanced at her watch. The alert briefing started at eight in the morning and was held in the main briefing room with crews from the other two squadrons. She headed that way.

She took her seat next to her crew commander, Fred Olsen. "How's the house coming?" he asked her.

"Slow, but it's a labor of love." Jackie felt fortunate to have Fred as a crew partner. He was patient, smart, and witty. Best of all, he lived down the road from her in Warrensburg with a wife who was an excellent cook. They watched out for her.

After weather, security, intelligence, and codes officers gave out information pertinent to that day and the next, Jackie and Fred went back to the Emergency War Order (EWO) vault to pick up the information that needed to be transported to the missile site. Jackie placed the taped-up classified material in the crew briefcase, securing it for the trip.

On her way out of the vault, she ran into Joel Perkins— literally. "Sorry. I wasn't watching where I was going," Jackie said, embarrassed.

"Don't worry about it," Joel said with a sly grin. "I'm not complaining."

Jackie watched as Joel's tall, broad-shouldered frame walked down the hallway. Joel was another young lieutenant missilier and also one of the few eligible bachelors in the squadron. His blond crew cut gave him a movie star look, with a smile that reached his eyes. She gave him an appreciative glance as she continued her way to the truck.

As they buckled in for their hour-trek to the missile site, Fred asked, "Are you still getting those calls?"

Jackie put the truck into gear and pulled out of the parking space. "Yep. If only he would talk dirty to me or something, at least I could get a laugh out of it. It's only silence."

"I don't think it's a joking matter. I think you should talk to the police. It's been going on, what, four weeks?"

"Six, but who's counting."

"Seriously. When we get back tomorrow, you need to go by the police station and ask them what they think you should do."

Chapter 5

True to her word, the next day after Jackie dropped off the government truck they'd driven home from the site, she headed straight to the Warrensburg Police Station. She felt a little self-conscious going to the police with such a minor issue, but if it would stop the calls and give her a good night's sleep, it would be worth a little embarrassment.

When the officer assigned to help her ushered Jackie into his office, Jackie explained the annoying calls. "And there's nothing consistent about them as far as I can tell," she finished up.

"And it sounds like a dead line?" the officer questioned.

"Yes. And they come at all hours of the night."

"None during the day?"

"Not that I can remember."

"Okay, here's what we are going to do. Take this paperwork over to the phone company on Harpers Street. This will authorize a phone trace on your line." He handed her the signed form. "They'll explain what you need to do once you get there."

Jackie thanked the officer and left. One more stop before heading home.

After finishing up with the phone company, Jackie returned home full of energy to pour into her house. As she approached the front porch, she noticed that the door from her bedroom to the large wraparound porch was ajar. She knew instantly this was not her forgetfulness. She had never used that door before. She couldn't have left it open.

She guardedly entered the opened front door and dropped her bags. "Keith? Are you here?" Jackie looked around the room and saw Keith had indeed been here while she was gone. The ceiling was replaced and painted, and his tools that had been strewn about on Wednesday were gone. Jackie continued through the house, noticing that each door was opened at least a crack. For some of the doors, that was quite a feat due to the stacks of unopened boxes along the walls. As Jackie walked through the house closing the doors, she silently cursed Keith for being so careless. She could understand wanting some airflow, but why did he need to open all seven doors? And why did he even go into the apartment off the back?

Frustrated with his insensitivity, Jackie picked up the kitchen phone and dialed Keith's number from the pad next to the phone.

"Hello?" Keith answered.

"Hey, this is Jackie. The ceiling looks great."

"Thanks."

"Was it really hot yesterday or something? You left all the doors open."

"What do you mean? I opened the front door, of course, but I didn't use any of the others."

Jackie was puzzled. "You didn't open them to air out the place while you worked?"

"No, there was no need to. And I was very careful to lock the door when I left after you told me about coming home to find the front door opened on Monday."

"Keith, I need you to change the locks on my doors."

∽

Jackie showed up at Kris and Alex's house, ready to relax. "I told you not to bring anything," Kris said as she took the bottle of wine out of Jackie's hands.

"No hunk in tow, so I brought the next best thing," Jackie said.

Kris led her into the kitchen where Alex was pouring himself a drink. "Can I get you anything?" he asked by way of a greeting.

"Wine would be great. Whatever's open."

Kris placed Jackie's bottle into the refrigerator to chill.

"Don't stand it up in there," Alex told Kris. "Lay it down so the cork stays wet." He reached behind her, taking the bottle out of her hand.

Jackie watched this interaction and wondered, not for the first time, how Kris and Alex ended up together. They seemed happy at times, but there was always tension in the air. Alex could be so harsh about little issues and was very negative about things that Kris found important. Jackie supposed it might be because Kris was in the Air Force and Alex wasn't. Jackie guessed it could be tough on a man, moving to support his wife's profession. A man who follows his wife's career is a reverse of the stereotype, and he probably didn't have many others to commiserate with.

Alex smiled at Jackie, handing her a glass of wine. He wasn't a bad-looking man, but Jackie wouldn't consider him good-looking either. He didn't seem to have much self-confidence, at times overcompensating as he tried to put on a good show. The shame was that it was often at Kris's expense.

"Mom and Dad are coming for a visit," Jackie told them, taking a sip of her wine.

"That's great," Kris said. "This'll be the first time they see the house, won't it?"

"Yeah, and I'm a little nervous about what Dad will say. He thought buying it was a bad idea."

"You'll prove him wrong," she said.

"You don't know my dad. He isn't easy to impress. Mom will love it though."

As they sat down to dinner, the talk turned to Jackie and her social life, or lack thereof. Kris thought Matt, Jackie's on-again-off-again boyfriend, was hot and wanted the most up-to-date scoop.

"There isn't much to tell," Jackie explained. "He's in Montana, I'm in Missouri. Not much chance for anything serious to happen that way."

Alex had to give his advice. "If that's how you feel, drop him and move on. Why waste your time?"

That's a guy for you, Jackie thought. *They think everything is simple and clear cut.*

It wasn't that easy for her. Jackie met Matt Burk during missile training at Vandenberg Air Force Base. His quick wit and handsome features made him fun to be around. They had started studying together early in the course, and one thing eventually led to another. The fact that he was intelligent, on top of everything else, had Jackie thinking hard about what a future with him would be like.

"I hate to throw away what we have," Jackie admitted to Kris.

"And what exactly is that?"

Jackie couldn't explain. Throughout high school and college, she'd kept all males at a distance. Getting too emotionally attached eventually led to the bedroom, and she wasn't ready for that. It had been drilled into her head since she was young that sex was saved for the marriage bed. How could she explain that after being so careful for twenty-three years, she threw it all away after too much to drink one Friday night?

At the time, she'd thought Matt was the one. The one who could understand her military lifestyle. The one who would always be there for her. The one who would wake up beside her every morning for the rest of her life.

Reality dealt her a tough blow when missile training was over; Matt went his way toward Malmstrom Air Force Base in Montana, and she went to Missouri. No mention of marriage. No talk of the future besides when they would get together next. The sex was not even what she expected it to be. Apparently she had read too many books. She expected electrifying and tender, not mechanical and to the point. But with all that, Jackie still couldn't let him go. After all, she had slept with him. In God's eyes that meant they were married, right?

"I'm not sure yet, okay?" Jackie answered Kris and Alex, but to herself she thought, *I'm not ready to admit failure.*

Chapter 6

Jackie had Saturday off which gave her a chance to clean before her parents arrived. She wasn't an overly messy person to begin with, but something about her parents put her into overdrive. It seemed she was always trying to impress them.

She went through the house, pushing tools to the side so her parents wouldn't trip over them. She couldn't pack everything away because her house was a work in progress.

When her parents arrived late that afternoon, the expression on her dad's face said it all—almost as if he'd taken a bite of a lemon. "Lot of work to be done," was his only comment.

Jackie knew she spent entirely too much time trying to please him. His years in the Army, and then as a police officer, had hardened him. Sometimes Jackie doubted he even knew how to show affection. If he did, he never let Jackie see it. Over six feet, Lawrence Austin towered over both Jackie and her mother. Jackie inherited more of his looks than her mother's. At one time he had brown hair; now it was mostly gray.

Her mother, Margaret, on the other hand, was spry and youthful looking. Her small-boned frame made her look smaller than Jackie although they were the same height. She wouldn't color her hair, but her natural reddish locks made what little gray she had look like highlights.

Jackie's mother hugged her. "You've done so much already.

I hardly recognize it from the photos you sent. How are you going to decorate the living room?"

They spent the rest of the evening walking through the house and brainstorming ideas for reconstruction and decorating.

The next morning, Jackie left the house by six for another alert. Her parents were still sleeping, but she knew they would enjoy looking around the town and spending time in the yard while she was gone. The weather had been beautiful lately.

To her surprise, when she returned the next day, she discovered her parents had been busy but not as tourists. They had finished patching the wall around the fireplace and had even hung the paneling.

"This is fantastic!" Jackie wrapped her dad in a bear hug. His discomfort didn't stop her.

"Well, we couldn't keep looking at it the way it was," he said.

"You saved me so much time!" Jackie admired the edging around the fireplace. The room was almost complete with the warm, brown paneling. She was still marveling over what a fantastic job they had done when her mother handed her the mail.

Jackie glanced through the bills quickly and came across a light blue envelope with her name and address typed. Curious, she opened it right away. She read it several times in disbelief. Jackie laughed and handed the letter to her mother. "Well, someone thinks I'm worth his attention."

Her mother took the letter and read it aloud.

"Roses are Red.
Violets are Blue.
There is no way to express,
How I feel about you."

Her mother looked up from the page. "Who's it from?"

"No idea. Obviously someone with too much time on his

hands . . . and not much creativity." She put the letter on the counter to be dealt with later. "Where are we going for dinner?"

That night, as Jackie was turning out the lights, the phone rang. "Hello?"

Empty air. Jackie resisted the urge to hang up at once. Instead she clicked the receiver and dialed *68 the way she had been instructed by the woman at the phone company. Hands shaking slightly, she hung up the phone. Picking up the pencil next to her bed, she wrote down the time and date. Then she clicked off the light, trying not to think of who might be making the calls.

~

Her parents had provided her a great distraction from work, her future, Matt, and men in general, but their departure forced Jackie to return to the real world and her normal routine. Having slept fitfully the night before, her mind full of worry about things she couldn't control, she now lay in bed thinking about her schedule for the day.

The competitors for Olympic Arena, the "Top Gun" of the missile world, were to be announced that afternoon. Olympic Arena, or OA as it was often called, was the dream of any career-minded person in the missile field.

Held at Vandenberg Air Force Base, California, many different specialties competed against their counterparts at other bases to determine who was best in their field. While the missiliers competed in the mock capsules fighting fires, monitoring maintenance on their mock missiles, and deciphering launch codes, security police fought off mock attackers, fired their weapons, and escorted missile transports.

Communications specialist and missile maintainers also plowed through their extensive technical orders to discover the mysterious bugs left behind by the evaluators. Then they rushed to correct the problem, ensuring the missiles were ready to launch under any circumstance. The competition results would be televised, and a lot of high-ranking people would be in attendance for score postings.

Grueling thirty-day OA training would begin for the chosen competitors within the month. Jackie couldn't decide if she was hoping to make the team for the sake of her career, or if she would be relieved not to see her name on the list and have one less thing to worry about. She had done well in the preliminary rounds of the competition held on base, so she knew she was in the running for the finals.

Jackie was roused from her thoughts by the phone ringing. "Hello?"

"Hi, Jackie. It's Louis. I was wondering if you wanted to get together for lunch today." Louis Meger was a fellow lieutenant who worked on base as a hospital administrator.

Louis was a nice guy but not exactly what Jackie was looking for in a relationship. He was fair-skinned and parted his reddish hair on the side. His freckles were one of the first things a person noticed about him because they were so prominent. He was physically attractive enough, but his neediness rubbed her the wrong way. He went out of his way to be accommodating. Jackie couldn't imagine ever arguing with him because he would give in just to be nice. That would take the fun out of it. She didn't want to give him any reason to get his hopes up about anything between them, but at the same time, she didn't want to hurt his feelings either.

"As long as it's a quick lunch, I think I could make it. I have a meeting at the squadron at thirteen-hundred."

"Sounds great. Want to meet at the Officers' Club?" Louis asked.

"Sure," Jackie answered. "I'll meet you there at twelve-fifteen."

Jackie hung up and finished getting ready for work. She needed some study time in the classified vault before her next training session.

As Jackie pulled into the Officers' Club, she saw Louis waiting for her at the curb. He had a big grin on his face. Jackie's stomach tightened into knots. *He's trying to be friendly*, she thought. *You need to lighten up a bit.*

Louis opened her car door and greeted her warmly. "I'm really glad you could make it on short notice. I had a lot of fun talking to you at the O-Club bar Friday night. I haven't been able to get you off my mind."

Uh-oh, Jackie thought. She couldn't quite put her finger on it, but she knew that nothing was going to click with this one. He was a little too intense.

"I had fun talking to you too," Jackie replied, although not as warmly. "We better be quick and eat so I'm not late for my meeting." Jackie led the way into the club as Louis hurried to get the door for her.

Jackie had to talk Louis out of paying for her meal, and as they finally made their way to a table in the dining room, Louis continued to smile and ask questions about Jackie and her interests.

Jackie was finally able to bring Matt up in conversation, "Well, I love to travel. As a matter of fact, Matt and I went to Belize a couple months ago."

"Matt?" Louis's eyes hardened.

"Oh, I thought I told you about him on Friday. We met at Vandenberg. He's a missilier at Malmstrom in Montana. We still see each other off-and-on but haven't decided how serious we want to get."

Louis's face lost its smile for a moment, and Jackie thought she saw a flash of anger in his eyes before he recovered, "Oh, you might have mentioned him before. It slipped my mind."

The rest of the meal was relatively silent, and Jackie tried to keep polite conversation going with questions of her own. Finally, it was time for her to go.

Louis walked Jackie to her car and opened the door. "I was thinking maybe we could go to a movie Friday night," Louis asked.

"My sister's coming to town tomorrow, but thanks anyway." Jackie slid behind the wheel.

"Well, maybe next weekend."

"Maybe," Jackie said gently as she closed the car door. "I'll see you around."

As Jackie pulled away, she wondered what was going on. She didn't remember college guys being this persistent. One *no* was enough to crush their ego, and they didn't ask her out again. There didn't seem to be as many guys interested in her either. Now she was asked out on a weekly basis. She didn't understand men and wasn't sure she liked all the attention.

Chapter 7

Parking at the squadron was hard to come by. A lot of people had turned out to see who would be selected as the missiliers for the Olympic Arena team. There would be four teams of two, but there were at least 140 people to choose from.

Jackie found a parking spot toward the back and rushed into the main briefing room. It was standing room only. The operations group commander got up and made a small speech, thanking everyone for trying out. Finally, the two captains assigned to train the teams were introduced, Captains Anderson and Nealy. Without further ado, the four teams were posted. Jackie saw her name on the screen, but it didn't register immediately. Her squadron mate sitting next to her elbowed her in the ribs, breaking her from her stupor.

Polite applause and congratulations all around were offered. Her new crew commander for the team, Captain Tim Blakely, caught her eye and gave her a thumbs-up.

Captain Anderson took the stage again. He waited for the room to quiet down. "We aren't allowed to start training until thirty days prior to Olympic Arena," he explained. "That should give us plenty of time to work out schedules and give the teams time to study on their own. We'll post a schedule as soon as we can. Thank you all for coming."

The group commander dismissed the room and more handshakes were offered. Jackie's head was spinning. She knew because she was the only second lieutenant on the list and one of only two females on the team, she would be watched closely for any screw-ups.

"Come on, star," Fred said, offering her a congratulatory handshake. "Just because you're on the elite team doesn't mean you don't have to pull your weight with the rest of us."

Jackie glanced at her watch. Weapons training was due to start in ten minutes. She hoped she would be able to focus.

"So, what's going on with your phone trace? Any results?" Fred asked as they walked back to the training area.

"No, I've been recording the time and date of the calls, but the phone company says I have to have thirty days' worth of information before they can make sense of it."

"Are the calls still coming?"

"Almost every other night. I'll be glad when we solve this riddle. It's probably a glitch in the phone system somehow."

Fred frowned. "I doubt that. You should be careful and not take this too lightly."

"It's not threatening, only annoying."

"For now," Fred added. "Who knows what this wacko is up to. Maybe you should get a dog."

Jackie laughed. "Yeah, that would be really fair with our schedule. It works for you because you have a wife that does all the work."

"True. Maybe a roommate?"

"I'll think about it. I can't imagine anyone would want to live in that construction zone."

W hen Jackie pulled up in front of her house, she noticed something white sticking out of her mailbox. She gathered her Technical Orders bag, TO bag for short, from the backseat and waited as a blue Ford Focus zipped past. Jackie crossed the street with a spring in her step.

It had finally hit her—she was on the Olympic Arena team!

After unlocking the front door and dropping her bags inside, Jackie returned to the mailbox on the front porch. In addition to the standard bills and advertisements, Jackie discovered the white thing sticking out of the mailbox was an envelope with her name typed on it and no return address. There wasn't even a postmark.

Jackie tucked the junk mail and bills under her arm and ripped open the curious envelope as she walked back into the house. She pulled out the small piece of stationery that contained a typewritten note.

I saw you from across the room.
My heart skipped a beat when you looked my way.
Was your smile meant for me?
No, not this time . . . but maybe the next.

Bizarre, Jackie thought as she tossed the junk mail onto the kitchen counter. She took the strange letter and the bills back to the study. She filed this second letter with the first one and started thinking about her next house project.

❧

A lison, I'm so glad you're here," Jackie said as she rushed to greet her sister. Although older, Alison was two inches shorter than Jackie. She had light hair and was built more like their mother. "How was the drive?"

Jackie guided Alison into the house and gave her the grand tour. Alison was duly impressed, fussing over the work Jackie had completed and enthusiastic about her plans for the next project.

"So, what do you have for me to do?" asked Alison, rolling up her sleeves. "I'm ready to work."

"Not today. You deserve a break after that fourteen-hour drive. We're going to dinner at my favorite place."

When Jackie and Alison pulled into the driveway, Kris was sitting on the front porch waiting for them. Kris and Alison hugged like old friends. Jackie had shared so many stories about Alison with Kris, and vice versa, that they felt as if they'd known each other for years.

The ladies followed Kris into the kitchen where she poured them each a margarita.

"Where's Alex?" Jackie asked.

"He's out of town on business," Kris explained. "That makes it just us girls. We can eat and drink as much as we want. You two can crash here tonight."

"To a girls' night," said Alison, raising her glass.

"To us," the other two agreed.

After dinner, the three settled on the back porch with a bottle of wine. Kris turned to Jackie. "Did you tell Alison about the love letters you've been getting?"

"Love letters? Do tell," Alison encouraged.

"They aren't really love letters. They're someone's idea of a bad joke—stupid poems sent anonymously in the mail."

"And you have no idea who it is?" Alison asked with concern.

"Not yet. But between the letters and the calls, I've started keeping a journal to see if I can figure out a pattern."

"A diary?" Kris asked with interest.

"No, not a diary." Jackie was adamant. "A journal to capture quick notes of things that happen on certain days. I definitely won't put anything personal in writing. Not with you around!"

Kris smiled mischievously as she thought best how to turn the tables on Jackie.

Pointedly ignoring Jackie, Kris asked, "So, Alison, what are we going to do to get Jackie's love life moving in the right direction?"

"I think the first step would be getting rid of her long-distance service, so she can't talk to Matt anymore."

"Agreed. We should also find a healthy substitute," Kris said.

"Do I get a say in this?" questioned Jackie.

"Not really," Alison replied. "Kris, there has to be someone in Missouri who will go out with Jackie."

"Oh, she has some to choose from, but her problem is she won't."

"Like who?" Jackie asked.

"There's Louis," answered Kris. "And Mike from the Five-Tenth squadron. Let's not forget about Joel. He's a great guy."

"Hmmm, tell me more." Alison refilled their wine glasses.

Before Kris had a chance to continue, Jackie broke in, "Louis isn't my type."

"Too nice," Kris slipped in.

Jackie shot her a dirty look and then went on. "Mike and I have gone to lunch, and he's sort of hot. Joel hasn't paid me much attention at all."

"He's paying attention, but you don't know what to do with it."

"This is silly."

Alison's face broke into a sly grin. "I know. Let's assign Jackie homework. She's good at doing what she's told. Maybe we need to tell her what to do."

Kris jumped at the idea. "Like a checklist! Missiliers love their checklists."

"What do you mean by a checklist?" Alison asked.

"You know, 'Identify good-looking man—check. Talk to good-looking man—check.'"

"Gotcha. I think we need to start slowly with Jackie," Alison continued as if Jackie wasn't there. "Little assignments at first so she can work her way up to a real relationship."

Jackie rolled her eyes at the conversation. "Are you two finished yet?"

"Not quite," Kris said, turning to her friend. "Your assignment, if you choose to accept it—"

"What if I don't?" Jackie countered.

"You already have," Kris continued. "In the next week, you must go on at least one date."

"Better give her two weeks—to be fair," Alison countered.

"Phone calls to Matt must be kept to a minimum. Twice a week at most," Kris stated determinedly. "I really think he's the reason you won't date. You're waiting for him to realize how lucky he is to have you. Give him up. He's nice, but he isn't into commitments. Hasn't he proven that to you already?"

Jackie didn't want to admit it, but Kris was probably right. She was still waiting for Matt to change his mind and begin a monogamous relationship with her. With his track record, why was she waiting?

"Okay. Agreed. But lunches count."

"Lunches count," agreed Alison and Kris in unison.

Chapter 8

Jackie was a little girl again. Running home from playing at the neighbor's, she was excited to tell Alison about the pet turtle her friend had received.

When she got to the back door, Jackie could hear Alison whimpering. Jackie crept forward to look through the screen door.

Their dad was sitting with his back to the door; her mom was sitting to his left. Alison was standing facing the door, holding something out in front of her.

Then Jackie heard her dad laugh. She could tell from that evil sound that he had been drinking. He drank beer every day, but it was when he drank the alcohol from the cabinet above the refrigerator that he was really mean.

"You think you're so grown up. Show me. Go ahead, take a deep breath," Jackie heard her father slur.

"No, Dad, please. I was only looking at them," Alison said.

Their dad shoved a lit cigarette into Alison's face, causing her to flinch. "I make the rules in this house," he said firmly.

Alison shook her head violently.

"Smoke it!" he demanded, this time putting the red tip dangerously close to her eye.

Alison took the cigarette out of his hand and put it to her lips. She was trembling as she obediently drew the caustic substance deep into her lungs. Her healthy, young organs rejected the foul air, causing Alison to cough desperately.

Her father slapped her face to make her stop. "You asked for it—now smoke it all."

When Alison picked her head up, she saw Jackie standing in the doorway. She quickly looked away. Jackie knew Alison didn't want her father's wrath to spread to include her little sister.

Jackie backed further into the shadows. Their mom was sitting there. *Why don't you do something?* Jackie wanted to scream at her.

"Make it glow," their father snarled.

Alison took another deep breath and gagged, letting the repugnant object drop from her trembling hand. Their dad laughed again until he saw the dropped cigarette. "Pick it up."

Alison did as she was told although there wasn't much left of the cigarette. As the burning tip got to her fingers, she looked for a place to deposit it.

"Now you'll see what a cigarette can really do." The man pinched Alison's fingers, trapping the cigarette butt between them. "Isn't this cool? Don't you wish your friends were here to see how cool you are?"

Alison began to beg as the glowing ember burned down. When the red-hot tip reached her fingers and singed her skin, she screamed.

"Don't you drop it!" her father yelled in her face, very angry now.

As the pain became too much, Alison turned her head and vomited. Jackie turned and ran away as fast as she could.

Jackie woke up sweating all over with her heart pounding. It took her a minute to remember she was still at Kris's house. She looked at the other couch and saw Alison sleeping peacefully. In this light, you couldn't see the scars on the fingers of her left hand.

Chapter 9

In the morning, Kris decided to help with Jackie's work projects, jumping in the backseat with a cooler of drinks and snacks.

"I do have food, you know," Jackie said.

"Sure, but you don't have what I brought." Kris pulled out chocolate-covered fruit, slices of cake, and wine coolers.

The girls laughed. "She does feed me better than you do," Alison said to Jackie.

When they got back to Jackie's house, it was still early, and there wasn't much activity on the street. A nest of young birds chirped noisily from the tree in the side yard. A cool breeze rustled the leaves and the nearest branches scratched on the tin roof covering the porch.

"Is it always this quiet?" Alison asked as they walked to the door.

"Usually. There are no young families with kids. It's mostly elderly people. There are a few college guys in that house." Jackie pointed to the little blue house with the neatly kept lawn. Then she nodded her head to the white house next door. "Mae lives there. She's looking forward to meeting you."

The girls went inside to start their first of many projects planned for the day. With Olympic Arena training starting soon, Jackie wouldn't have much opportunity to work on the house for a while.

As Jackie pulled out the equipment they'd need for their tasks, Alison watched her. "You've grown up so much."

"It was bound to happen," Jackie said. She took Kris's cooler and headed to the kitchen.

Alison stared after her.

"What's the strange look for?" Kris asked.

Alison shook her head. "The Air Force has been really good for Jackie. Growing up, she spent so much energy trying to please people. She never felt she was good enough—especially when it came to our father."

"Is he really that hard on her? I've heard her make references about him but haven't seen them interact."

"The kicker is that Jackie is good at everything she tries— she just doesn't see it. For some reason, she needs Dad to acknowledge her accomplishments, almost as if that's all that counts."

Kris thought about it. "That's a shame. She's doing great in the squadron. This missile competition is a huge deal, but I'm not sure anyone outside the career field would really understand it."

Alison talked as she searched through the pile of equipment looking for something. "In high school, Jackie played volleyball on the varsity team as a freshman. She wasn't very tall, but she could jump. It always bothered her that she was a setter and not a hitter, but in that case, nothing but height was stopping her. She practiced relentlessly. We even set up a net in the backyard where she spent hours practicing her footwork as she approached the net to hit the ball."

Pulling out a paint scraper, Alison positioned herself in the dining room where the wallpaper was practically falling off the wall and started scraping. Kris joined her, peeling away the largest pieces with her hands, dropping them into a nearby trash can.

Alison continued her story, "There was a championship game Jackie's junior year. It was a tie game and a tied match. Each team had won two games, making this their fifth game of the afternoon. Jackie was serving. She had a hard overhand that she could place exactly where she wanted—I would know because she smacked the ball at me hours on end in the backyard."

Kris smiled.

"Jackie tossed the ball and served beautifully into a hole on the other side. The score was now fifteen to fourteen, but they needed to win by two. When Jackie was in her game, she was totally focused. If you didn't know her, you would think she was mad. Her teammates knew better and rolled with it.

"Just before her hand connected on the next serve, the other team slipped in to cover the hole where Jackie had aimed. The ball bounced off an opposing girl's arms. Jackie had run into position near the net to prepare to take the second hit as the setter. The other team's hitter smacked the ball straight down near the outside line. Jackie dove backward, slipping her arms between the ball and the floor, popping it up perfectly near the net. The other team was caught off guard. They never expected that anyone could have returned their hardest hitter's shot, let alone set it up for a spike on the first hit." Alison paused as she scraped the paper from the corner.

She wiped the hair off her forehead with the back of her hand. "Jackie's teammate jumped at the ball and took a fake swing, causing the other team's blockers to jump. At the same time, a second girl jumped behind the first hitter and gently dinked the ball to fall at the feet of the blockers. Game and match point—it was a fantastic play! All because Jackie was able to receive that first hit."

"Sounds like Jackie was a pretty good player," Kris said.

"Absolutely! And everyone knew it. The stands were cheering wildly, and the girls were all clapping her on the back. Jackie was grinning from ear to ear. I saw her looked up to where Mom and I were sitting. Then her face fell; I knew it was because she didn't see Dad. When she finally found him in the crowd, he was standing at the gym door, leaning very close to Jackie's trigonometry teacher, whispering something. I saw the teacher blush and laugh; I'm sure Jackie did too. Our dad was oblivious to the great play Jackie had just made."

"Ouch," Kris said.

"Ouch is right. Jackie's face fell. She was crushed that he was paying attention to some other woman rather than watching her play."

"What about you? Did you fight for his attention?"

Alison shook her head. "I gave up a long time ago trying to win his approval. But Jackie would never give up; it's not in her nature. More than anything, she wanted Dad to compliment her."

Jackie came back into the room, and Alison stopped talking.

Jackie eyed them curiously. "Did I interrupt something?"

"Nothing important," Kris said. "Just trying to figure out how hard you're going to work us before we can get a break."

"A break? You haven't even started yet."

"Sure we have—look!"

"Finish the room, and you can take a break." Jackie indicated the large area they had to cover. It would take them hours to prepare the walls enough for painting.

Kris threw a large sheet of wallpaper she had just pulled off the wall in Jackie's direction.

Jackie swatted it away. "Now you have a mess to clean up too."

Kris stuck her tongue out at Jackie, causing Alison to laugh at their antics.

∽

W hen do you work next?" Alison asked Jackie, turning her attention back on the peeling wallpaper.

"Seventeen-hundred, day after tomorrow." Jackie grabbed another scraper and attacked a different section of wall.

"Seventeen-hundred? Why can't you tell time like normal people?"

Jackie looked up at her sister. "Sorry, it's a habit. Once you get used to it, military time is really easy. Think of a twenty-four-hour cycle instead of two twelves. Oh-seven-hundred is seven a.m.; eleven-hundred is eleven a.m. After noon, you keep going up. One p.m. is thirteen-hundred; two p.m. is fourteen-hundred. So if you ever get confused on the p.m. times, subtract twelve."

Alison started laughing. "Right. In case it ever comes up in conversation with anyone other than you two!"

As the ladies finished removing the last of the wallpaper layers, Jackie heard the creaky sounds of the steps on her front porch. "Mailman," she said, moving to the front of the house. She was becoming accustomed to the noises of her old house.

She came back into the dining room flipping through the mail. When her eyes found an envelope with her name and address typed but no return address, she put the other mail aside and turned her attention to opening it. Jackie chuckled as she started to read out loud,

> *"Your hair frames your face.*
> *You move with style and grace.*
> *And in the pale starlight,*
> *Your eyes dance with delight."*

Her voice faltered.

"What's wrong?" Alison asked.

"This is starting to get weird." Jackie continued reading.

> *"With whom will you share your secret ways?*
> *Does Michael really deserve your praise?*
> *A lunch with Louis is just fine,*
> *But with Joseph you'll drink white wine?*
> *With Joel, you seek more time.*
> *Is he the next one in the line?"*

Kris took the letter from Jackie's hand, reading it quickly. "Jackie, he's been watching you."

Chapter 10

He spied the young lady approaching him down the aisle. *She's interesting*, he thought. *Good-looking, not self-conscious.* As she drew closer, he was pleased to see that she had no wedding ring.

He caught her eye, smiled, and returned his gaze to the paint can he was inspecting. Out of the corner of his eye, he saw her stop. She, too, was examining a selection of paints.

"What do you think of this color?" he asked her, holding up a can of military green paint.

The petite woman smiled at him, answering hesitantly, "Well, it's a bit dark for my taste, but it depends on where you're going to use it, I suppose."

The man put the can back. "You're right. Thanks. It always helps to have a beautiful lady's opinion."

She rewarded him with a bright smile.

"So what are you working on?" he asked, feigning interest.

"I just moved in so I'm repainting. You wouldn't believe the colors they had in the kitchen." The woman continued to search through the color palettes, but he knew she was more interested in him.

"Just moved? From where?"

"California. Never thought I would find myself in the Midwest," she answered.

"So why are you in the Midwest?" he asked. *It's easy to get women to talk. All you need to do is make them feel important. The subject is irrelevant.*

She shrugged, turned her body more to face him. "I wanted to try something different, so when I was offered a teaching job at Central Missouri State, I took it. It'll be interesting for a while. I'll play it by ear whether or not I stay."

"You probably haven't had much of a chance to see the area. I would be happy to show you around," he offered.

She gave him a coy look. "I think I'd like that."

I'm sure you will, he thought.

Chapter 11

Alison and Jackie decided to change into shorts and t-shirts to go for a walk before Alison had to head for home. As Alison turned to reach for her shirt, Jackie caught sight of the ugly scars on her back. Every time she thought about them, Jackie felt enraged and even a little helpless.

Alison turned back and caught Jackie staring. "I don't blame him, you know," Alison said quietly.

Jackie shook her head and turned away. "Why not? Why don't you hate him?" Her inner voice asked, *Why don't I hate him?*

"First of all, forgiveness doesn't leave room for hate. Second, because he's our father. We wouldn't be who we are without him. He's made some mistakes—pretty big ones. But he isn't a bad man. He went through some tough times himself growing up. He did the best he could with us."

"That's bullshit." Jackie couldn't let go of the resentment she was feeling. Pulling on her t-shirt, she sat down to put on her shoes.

Alison finished dressing and grabbed her shoes. Sitting to face Jackie, she continued. "Jackie, I believe everything happens for a reason. You might not know or understand the reason right away—or ever—but there's still a reason."

Jackie was unconvinced.

"Remember when we were little, and you lost your coat when we were playing outside by the pond?" Alison asked.

Jackie nodded, "It was my favorite one. Mom sewed patches all around the bottom to decorate it."

"You were grounded for a week and sent to bed without supper."

"I remember. You snuck me food," Jackie said with a mischievous grin.

Alison went on, "But Monday morning at school we saw Noa Burns wearing your coat. Her family was so poor she usually came to school without one, even in the snow. Remember?"

"Sure." Jackie could finally see where Alison was going with this.

"You lost your coat for a reason—so Noa could have it. And as I recall, you never told Mom and Dad that you saw Noa with your coat."

"No, I didn't. I didn't want them to try to get it back. Even though Mom refused to sew patches on my new jacket."

"So, you see? Things happen for a reason. What happened to me when I was younger has made me a stronger person now. Like what has happened to you has made you a stronger person. Where do you think you get your determination from? Who in their right mind would buy a hundred-year-old house with no air conditioning or shower?"

Jackie laughed. "I fixed the shower!" It was good to be able to talk to Alison like this. She could dig around inside Jackie's brain, pulling out the right answers.

"I guess we turned out all right," Jackie admitted.

Jackie heard the telephone ring and headed for the phone in her bedroom. This had become routine as the hang-ups had increased. She kept her notepad next to the bed, so she could write down the date and time before she forgot it.

Jackie picked up the phone without saying anything.

"Hello?" came the questioning voice on the other end.

"Uh, hello, sorry. I'm here," Jackie stammered.

"Hi, this is Louis. I was wondering if you wanted to catch a bite to eat. I heard you aren't on the schedule tomorrow."

Instinctively Jackie started to say no, but then she remembered the deal she'd made with Kris and Alison. Alison was getting ready to leave, so there was no reason to put this off. "That sounds good," she said.

Louis sounded pleased. His response was eager. "When should I pick you up?"

"Give me a couple hours. My sister is still here."

"Sounds great. See you then!"

Jackie stared at the phone for a minute thinking, *I never told him where I lived . . .*

Wednesday morning, Jackie went in early to check the schedule for the next week and noticed her crew pairing had been switched. She was now crewed with Captain Tim Blakely—also her crew commander for Olympic Arena. *Well, officially, training hadn't started, but there was no reason they couldn't start learning how each other's minds worked.*

Tim was short and stocky with thinning brown hair. His oval-shaped glasses and serious expression completed his intellectual look. Those that got to know him knew he was quick to smile and to make others smile. Tim had been on crew for over three years and was well respected around the squadron. He was a calm, quiet thinker, which would balance Jackie's impulsive, shoot-from-the-hip reactions.

Jackie dutifully headed to Kris's office to report on her date with Louis. It had been nice once Louis had gotten over his initial awkwardness. They laughed as they shared different stories from the missile world and the medical community. She and Louis were very different, but Air Force life gave them common ground. But she still didn't feel any attraction toward him. He had moments of urgent clinginess that made her uncomfortable.

As she came through Kris's doorway, she saw Joel sitting in front of the desk.

"Hi, Jackie, come on in." Kris beckoned to a chair nearby.

"It's not important. I can come back later."

"No, come in. You know Joel, don't you?"

Joel smiled as Jackie approached. "Sure, we've met a few times," Joel said as he stood and extended his hand.

Jackie took his hand for a moment and then sat in the offered chair.

"So what brings you in today?" Kris asked Jackie.

"I'm going to do some studying in the vault."

"Me too," said Joel. "Maybe we could study together? That is if the Olympic Arena team is allowed to associate with us lesser folk." Again, the smile.

And what a nice smile, Jackie thought. "I guess I could bring myself to impart some of my wisdom upon you," she joked with a poor English accent.

"Let's go," Joel said, rising from his seat.

As Jackie got up to leave, Kris asked, "Was there something you were coming in to see me about, Jackie?"

"Nothing I can't tell you later," she said with a wink that went unseen by Joel.

Y ou went out with him?" Kris sounded genuinely surprised. "It's no big deal. We went to the batting cages," Jackie said, "although Joel's not much of a baseball player." With a sheepish grin, she added, "I think I embarrassed him."

"You probably hit better than he did."

Jackie laughed. "Now that you mention it . . . "

"Have you told Alison yet?"

"I just got off the phone with her before I called you. She's proud of her little sister."

"Okay, you've exceeded your one date in two weeks. But how are things going with Matt?"

"I've talked to him a few times," Jackie admitted. "It's actually kind of fun because he called at least two of the four times I've been out and quizzes me on where I've been."

"Did you tell him?"

"Not directly. I mentioned going out with friends or seeing a particular movie, but I don't say who I was with."

"That's got to be eating him up."

"Serves him right. Who knows how many girls he's been sleeping with since I saw him last."

"Has he mentioned coming to visit?"

"He asked, but I told him I have to check my schedule and get back to him."

"I think you're starting to get it, girl."

The next day Jackie didn't have anything on the schedule except a trainer ride at three p.m. On her way to work, she pondered why they called it a "ride" when obviously the mock capsule wasn't going anywhere. Left over from the pilots, she supposed. Still, this was the most worthwhile training because it was hands-on and fairly realistic. Where else could you practice decoding launch orders and turning keys?

After her trainer ride, Jackie drove home in silence. She had a lot to think about. The instructors had certainly stepped-up the level of knowledge needed for this ride. She'd made her share of mistakes, but so had Tim. She knew she needed to put in more study time before they met again. She didn't want to let her partner down.

Jackie parallel parked in front of her house. She reached into the back seat and grabbed her TO bag. She grunted as she heaved it out. Was it her imagination or was the bag getting heavier? Maybe she was getting weaker from not working out . . . and she was exhausted.

Jackie crossed the street and strode up the short walk to her house. Before she reached the porch, she noticed the screen door to her bedroom was open.

"Now what?" Jackie said out loud in exasperation. As she drew closer, she could tell that only the screen was open, not the door itself. *That's a relief*, she thought.

Wedged in the doorway was a large box. Jackie set her crew bag on the porch and pulled the box out. There was a note on it: *I would give you the world.*

She turned the knob on the door—still locked. She gave a relieved sigh. It was from her admirer, not the break-in artist. Jackie carefully unwrapped the package, not even wanting to take it inside before knowing what it was. A world globe. *How poetic.* Unlocking the front door, she retrieved her crew bag and the package and went inside.

Olympic Arena training was due to start on Monday—two more days of freedom, if you could call it that. Jackie felt as if she were starting to recite her technical orders in her sleep. As she closed her books for the night and reached over to shut off the light, the phone rang. She glanced at the clock. It was already after midnight. Even Matt wouldn't be calling this late.

"Hello?" Nothing. "Hello?" Jackie dutifully pressed the *, six, and eight keys, put the phone down, entered the date in her log, shut off the light, and closed her eyes. She was asleep in no time.

Sometime later, the shrill ring of the telephone invaded her dreams. Jackie woke up slowly. Picking up the phone, she said groggily, "Hello?" Nothing. *What's up with this?* Jackie was annoyed. It was three in the morning.

Slamming the phone down, she rolled over to go back to sleep. Fifteen minutes later the phone rang again. Jackie considered taking the phone off the hook but knew she wasn't supposed to do that because she was on standby for alert. She could be called in at any time if someone was unable to go out to the capsule, and she would have to go in their place. She picked up the phone and hung it up without bothering to answer it. She made the appropriate notation on the paper next to her bed without bothering to turn on the lights.

Chapter 12

Jackie spent the next afternoon studying before heading off to play volleyball. She knew it didn't count as real exercise, but it was a good release.

Although she didn't know all their names, the gang she met up with at the gym was made up of excellent players, and she was improving her game just being on the court with them.

When she walked into the gym at four, she noticed Joel lifting weights. Catching his eye, she waved as she walked onto the volleyball court. She still had a smile on her face when she rounded the corner.

Uh-oh, she thought, checking out the players warming up. *Since when did Louis start showing up for these scrimmages?*

"Hi, Jackie. Ready to play?" Louis asked from across the gym.

"Be there in five minutes," she answered as she pulled out her court shoes. Eight other players were already on the court. Should be a good practice.

Sometime during their second game, Jackie got the feeling someone was watching her. Turning to the bleachers, she saw Joel sitting in the stands. He smiled. Jackie turned her attention back to the game, concentrating on not messing up in front of him.

By the time they had finished playing, Joel was gone but Louis was waiting to talk to her. "Want to catch a bite to eat?" he asked hopefully.

"No, thanks," Jackie replied. "I have some work to do at home."

Louis was taken aback by her abruptness but tried to play it off. "Well, if you ever need any help, give me a call. I can be pretty handy around the house."

"Thanks. I'll keep that in mind." Jackie changed her shoes quickly and headed for the door.

S unday came and went. Jackie realized all too soon that she wasn't ready for the next thirty days. At six o'clock Monday morning, she was already on base and was dragging.

"What's wrong with you?" Joel asked, concern in his voice when he saw her walk through the door into the squad room.

"The phone kept ringing in the middle of the night, waking me up."

"Who would be calling you that late?" he asked.

"Wish I knew. It's been going on for months."

"That's crazy. Just take your phone off the hook," he suggested.

"Can't do that. We have to be on call."

Joel shook his head. "That sucks. Well, if you need a good night's sleep, you can always crash at my house," he offered.

Jackie looked up at him suspiciously.

Joel put his hands up in defense. "No, I mean in the guest room. Promise."

Smiling, she answered, "Thanks. I'll think about it. For now, I need to get going. Olympic Arena training officially starts today."

"Good luck. I'm heading out on alert, so maybe I'll see you when I get back."

Jackie waved and headed for the second-floor office space that was set aside for the four two-person teams. It wasn't much bigger than the office Kris had to herself downstairs, but something was better than nothing.

The bulletin board on the back wall was filled with wiring diagrams, schedules, and references. *This may be our first day, but the instructors obviously started preparing long before now,* Jackie surmised.

"We only have thirty days," Captain Anderson reminded them for what seemed the hundredth time. "Here are your schedules. When you're not in the trainer, we expect you to be in the EWO vault studying."

Jackie looked at the schedule. At least they had given them Sundays off, but the rest of the days were going to be long—starting at six or seven in the morning most days and not finishing until ten at night. *How am I going to keep up this schedule?*

~

A week into the grueling schedule and Jackie was already feeling run down. Not only was the pace maddening, but she was also no longer allowed gym time. The trainers felt that if someone saw her working out at the gym, they would assume she was not taking her training for Olympic Arena seriously enough. Perception is everything in the military.

As she crawled into bed slightly before midnight, the phone rang. "Hello?" Nothing. *Not again,* Jackie thought. She hung up the phone and pulled the covers over her head.

At two in the morning, the phone rang again. Jackie picked up the phone but didn't say anything. It didn't sound like anyone was there. She hung up. Then she took the phone off the hook and shoved it under her bed. She wasn't in the mood to deal with this tonight.

When Jackie awoke at six, she put the phone back on the hook, placing it on her nightstand. It rang almost instantly.

"Hello?"

"Jackie? Who have you been talking to all morning? I've been trying to reach you for an hour." It was Tim.

"No one. I was getting prank calls in the middle of the night, so I took my phone off the hook. What's up?"

"They moved our trainer to first thing this morning. We need to be there by six-thirty. Are you going to make it?"

Jackie glanced at the clock. "It'll be tight, but I'll be there. Thanks for the call."

"Taking your phone off the hook probably isn't the right answer for the prank calls," Tim warned.

"I know. See you soon." Jackie hung up, heading toward the bathroom. The phone rang again. "Hello?" Nothing. Jackie slammed the phone down went into the bathroom before the phone had a chance to ring again.

Jackie, how's OA training going?" Fred Olsen asked as he passed her in the squadron hall.

"Tough, but definitely a learning experience," Jackie answered. "I just got raked over the coals during a trainer."

Olsen patted her on the back as he continued down the hall. After a few steps, he stopped and looked back at her. "Whatever happened to the phone trace the police were doing for you?"

"You know, with this schedule, I haven't had a chance to make it to the telephone company to follow up on it. I turned in my times and notes a week or so ago."

"You need to make it a point to go in," Fred admonished.

"I'll talk to Captain Anderson today," she promised.

She went into the training room, dropping her books onto a desk. As she pulled out the first technical order and started to read, Captain Anderson came into the room.

"Good morning, lieutenant."

"Good morning, sir." Jackie thought about the best way to broach the subject but couldn't think of one. She decided direct was the only option.

"Sir, I need to go into Warrensburg this afternoon for a little while."

"Why?" he asked sharply.

"I have to make a stop at the phone company."

"Can't you do that after work?"

She took a deep breath and went on. "They'll be closed by the time we finish here."

Captain Anderson mumbled something under his breath and stalked out of the room.

Jackie took that as permission, figuring she could get to Warrensburg and back if she didn't stop to eat.

During lunch, Jackie quickly drove to the telephone company office. She asked for the person in charge of phone traces.

The waiting room was depressing with peeling wallpaper and cracked tiles on the floor. This company had seen better days.

After waiting a precious ten minutes of her thirty-minute lunch break, a young woman wearing high heels and a gray skirt appeared at the doorway. She looked at Jackie with undisguised annoyance. "Are you Miss Austin?"

"Lieutenant Austin. Yes, that's me," Jackie said, coming to her feet.

"Lieutenant Austin, we don't have any records on file that a phone trace was supposed to be accomplished."

"What do you mean? I brought the papers over myself. The receptionist explained what I was supposed to do. She said to come back in thirty days." People in the waiting room turned to stare as Jackie spoke.

"I'm sorry. We don't have any paperwork to that effect. If you want to file with the police department and bring the paperwork to me, I will—"

But Jackie cut her off. "You mean I've been going through this hell for the past forty, sleepless nights for nothing?"

"Miss, if you will—"

"Don't you people know you're messing with people's lives here? This is not a routine maintenance call. Someone is harassing me!" Jackie was starting to tremble now. Her anger and fear were mixing into a lethal combination. Before she exploded, Jackie turned and stormed out of the office. "Idiots!" she blasted to no one in particular.

When she returned to the base, Captain Anderson was waiting for her at the office door. "Where have you been? You're ten minutes late."

"I told you I had things to do. Some of us do have a life, you know," Jackie snapped as she grabbed her books and marched out the door.

Anderson turned to where Blakely was studying his technical orders. "What's her problem?"

"Jackie has been getting nuisance calls and unsettling letters. She's under a lot of pressure."

"Well, she's acting pretty unprofessional. Maybe she needs to go see somebody about her issues. We can't afford her cracking up on us during the competition."

Chapter 13

Okay. I'm here. Now what?" Jackie said.

"That depends. What do you expect?" the base counselor responded.

"Anderson must think this is pretty important if he released me from study time to talk to you. But you better heal me quickly, because I only have an hour." Jackie exaggerated looking at her watch.

Captain Daniel Evans smiled warmly. "No pressure there."

Jackie sighed. "I've been receiving phone calls—hang-ups really—for a couple of months now. They wake me up at all hours and that makes me grumpy. This schedule for OA is painful. A common day is oh-seven-hundred until twenty-two-hundred. It's ridiculous."

"What do you do to unwind?"

"What do you want to hear? Am I drinking? The answer is no. Well, not in the way you mean. I have a glass of wine sometimes, but it isn't a problem. Maybe it would help. Alcohol puts me to sleep."

"If you weren't in this competition, what would you do to unwind?"

"I don't unwind."

"You must do something."

"Work on my house, play volleyball, work out at the gym."

"I've seen you before on the court. You're pretty good," Daniel commented. He watched her closely, but she didn't respond.

"So tell me what's really going on," he said finally.

Jackie sighed, frustrated. "I told you. I'm getting harassing phone calls that are interrupting my sleep. Between that and the training schedule, I'm exhausted. Maybe if I could use this hour to catch a quick nap, that would do me some good."

He smiled at her lame joke. "Then let's talk about something else besides work."

Eventually Jackie relaxed, falling into an easy conversation with him. She talked about Alison and her family. She told him about her house, pride evident in her voice. When the hour was over, Jackie was surprised that she had talked so much. She stood up, asking, "Am I cured?"

"I think you're on your way," Daniel offered.

As Jackie turned to go, she hesitated, turning back to Daniel to ask, "Some of us are getting together to play volleyball on Sunday if you want to join us. We'll be at the base gym at sixteen-hundred."

"Maybe I'll see you there." He took her hand, holding it a little longer than Jackie thought was necessary.

⌒

Sunday morning was beautiful, mostly because Jackie didn't have to get up and go to work. As she lay in bed thinking about everything she wanted to accomplish that day, her planning was interrupted by thoughts of Daniel. *Strange*, Jackie thought when she caught herself—*Daniel and not Joel . . . or Matt.*

She resigned herself to start the day. She pulled a t-shirt over her head, going barefoot into the dining room. "Where shall I start?" she said, looking around.

She decided it was time to replace the ceiling in the dining room. Although messy, she found that the easiest way to remove the old plaster was to knock it down by hitting it with a steel rod, then getting out of the way when chunks crashed to the floor. *Might as well get to it*, Jackie thought as she went to get her tools.

Just after three o'clock, Jackie quickly showered and changed into her gym clothes. She grabbed her court shoes, carefully locking the door behind her. Her shoulders were a little sore from shoveling the chunks of plaster into the wheelbarrow and carting it to the street, but it was a good kind of sore. Jackie knew she was getting a great workout, in addition to improving her real estate investment. Getting to play volleyball was her treat to herself. It would be refreshing to talk to non-missiliers for a change.

As Jackie concentrated on setting the ball in exactly the right place for the hitters, she was surprised to see Daniel next in line to hit. He tossed her the ball. She set the ball close to the net, then stood back and watched as he gracefully approached, jumped, and slammed the ball hard onto the other side. "Nice hit," everyone said almost as one.

The match was good. Only twelve people had turned out, so no one had time for a break. In between games, the players mixed up the teams to practice with different people, but everyone was fairly evenly matched. Jackie enjoyed watching Daniel on the court. He had certainly played before. And his light-hearted comments and friendly flirtations added another level of excitement to the game.

By six-thirty, people started to leave. Jackie was hesitant to go but knew she needed to study. As she said her goodbyes, she walked to the stands to change her shoes. When she looked up, Daniel was standing in front of her.

"Want to grab something to eat?"

"Sure," Jackie answered, quickly forgetting her need to study.

Chapter 14

Who's our vic?" Police Lieutenant Jackson didn't waste time on small talk.

Sergeant Marcus replied as efficiently. "Betsy Latin, age twenty-five, professor at Central Missouri State in the Literature Department. Moved to Sedalia a few months ago. Not married, no family in the area."

Jackson looked around the room. There wasn't much sign of a fight. The furniture was all in place except for a few couch cushions on the floor.

Marcus led the way into the bedroom. The lab techs were hunched over the body, taking pictures and collecting evidence. Jackson noted the absence of decorations and the sparse furnishings in the room, only a double bed, and a dresser. The girl was sprawled on the floor near the window, the early morning sunlight accentuating the blood on her back.

"The victim was struck on the head and fell here. Then it looks like she was stabbed repeatedly while she was down," Marcus observed. "After the first blow, she probably lost consciousness. You can see the crushed skull from here."

"Then why stab her over and over?" Jackson wondered aloud. "What's the point?"

"Pissed him off?" Marcus offered. "He wants her to get up and fight, but she doesn't?"

Jackson nodded. It was a sound theory, but at this point, they could only guess. "What did she do to get on his bad side?"

Chapter 15

How are you holding up?" Kris asked when Jackie came slumping into her office.

"I'm here, but my head hurts."

Kris pulled some Motrin out of her desk drawer and tossed it to Jackie. "Have you eaten yet?"

"No, I was coming to see if you wanted to grab a bite. I only have half an hour."

"Let's go," Kris said, grabbing her purse and heading for the door. "You need to keep up your strength."

After they had picked out their sandwiches and were seated at a table, Kris started with her questions.

"Well?"

"Well what?" Jackie tried not to smile as she took a bite of her sandwich.

"Tell me the latest on Joel. Does he make your toes tingle? I want all the details."

"Do I look like the type who would kiss and tell?"

"Only to your best friend," Kris said.

"Besides, when would I have time to kiss?"

Kris gave her a disbelieving look. "Don't give me that. I see him waiting for you when you get here in the morning. And I'll bet you've seen him a few times after your late nights."

Jackie blushed. "He has been helping me study," she admitted.

"Yeah, right!"

"Really!" Jackie protested. "Sometimes he brings dinner to the training room, so we can eat while going over checklists."

"And I'm sure that's all he brings you," Kris teased.

"Now that you mention it . . . he is a good kisser, but that's it—no sparks."

"But he's gorgeous!" Kris was incredulous.

Jackie laughed. "Looks aren't everything. I still like being around him. I don't think I want it to go any further. I don't have time with my schedule anyway."

"Does he know that?"

"I haven't told him, but I'm not encouraging him." Jackie glanced at her watch. "Let's get out of here. I can't be late again."

I'm checking in, like the doctor ordered," Jackie said into the phone.

"I appreciate it," Daniel answered. "It keeps me from having to chase you down. It's so much easier when my patients follow orders."

She heard the smile in his voice.

"So, how's the training going?" he asked.

Jackie cradled the phone between her head and shoulder as she continued to flip through her technical orders. "It's going okay. The trainers are assholes at times. They act like this is life or death."

Daniel chuckled. "Those who can't do—teach. Are you at work now?"

"Yep. Since oh-seven-hundred this morning."

"That's got to stink on the weekends."

She smiled. "Oh, is it a weekend? I hadn't noticed." Talking to Daniel was so easy. "You doing anything fun this weekend?"

"I'm working around the house. I want to get the floors sanded so I can stain them."

"Sounds like a big job."

"Are you offering?" Daniel asked.

"Maybe . . . I couldn't help 'til tomorrow though. I have a trainer later this afternoon."

"Of course, I wouldn't expect anything less. Call me on Sunday when you wake up. Breakfast is on me."

"I'm in. Talk to you then." Jackie hung up, a broad smile on her face. Not truly a date, but at least a connection.

Saturday evening, Jackie arrived home shortly after dusk following a late afternoon in the training simulator. She made her way carefully up the steps of her porch, listening to the creak with every step. *Part of the house's charm,* she thought with a smile.

Jackie dropped her crew bag, unlocked the door, and reached inside to turn on the light. Nothing happened. She could no longer convince herself that these quirks associated with the house were due to her forgetfulness. Without a second thought, she ran as fast as she could manage in the dark to the home of her old crew partner, Fred. Thankfully he was only a block away.

His wife Katie answered the door. Her smile quickly faded at the look of distress on Jackie's face. "What's wrong?"

Jackie's eyes flicked from Katie back to her door, checking to see if she had been followed. Willing her voice to be calm, she asked, "Ah, is Fred around?"

"Come in. I'll get him."

Fred's bulky figure came into the living room with a beer in his hand. He saw her restlessness. "What's happened?"

"It's probably nothing," Jackie said dismissively. "My lights won't work. Can you come down and help me get the electricity turned back on?"

"Sure. Let me grab a flashlight."

Jackie and Fred walked back down the street to her house. The night was cool and dark. There was no moon to light their way, and the city hadn't invested money for street lights on these little side streets. They walked carefully following the beam of Fred's flashlight.

The door was still ajar. They stepped cautiously over the threshold. Fred walked into the darkness, trying other light switches throughout the house. "Where's your fuse box?" he called from the interior.

"On the screened-in porch off the kitchen," Jackie answered, moving toward the sound of his voice.

Fred took one look in the box and turned his flashlight toward Jackie, careful not to shine it in her face. "You probably don't want to hear this, but your fuses are missing."

"What do you mean missing?"

"I mean someone took them out. They aren't here."

Jackie was visibly shaken. "Now what do we do?"

"Let's go buy more. Then I think you need to call the police."

Jackie went along in silence as Fred drove to the store, picked out the fuses, and returned to Jackie's house. He replaced the fuses and then walked through the entire house, looking in every closet and behind every door while Jackie called the police.

The police officers arrived within ten minutes and listened as Jackie related her story. She also told them about coming home to open doors in the past weeks.

"Ma'am, how long was this house vacant before you moved in?" asked one of the officers.

"About six months," Jackie replied.

The officers shared a look, then the second officer said, "I think someone is playing with you—most likely kids. You said that the doors were left open, but nothing was taken."

Jackie nodded her head.

"Then, when you changed the locks, the fuses were taken off the back porch—an area that's not locked."

Again, Jackie agreed.

"Well, some kids must have had a key to this place or were able to pick the locks. They were probably having fun scaring the new person on the block. When you changed the locks on them, they couldn't get in anymore, so they resorted to removing your fuses. Since the kitchen porch is screened in, they would have easy access without anyone noticing. I suggest that you get a lock for the back porch."

Jackie debated telling the police about the phone calls. She was still angry that the phone trace hadn't worked and didn't want the cops to think she was overreacting to children's pranks, so she kept her mouth shut.

Before they left, Fred and the police officers helped Jackie move heavy furniture to block all the outside doors except the front door, so she would feel safer. The officers told her to be sure to call them right away if anything else strange happened.

"We'll be patrolling the neighborhood."

"You can always call me," Fred offered. "I'm going to go fill Katie in. She's probably worried."

Jackie thanked them, bolting the door after they left.

She lay in bed staring at the ceiling. All this was too unreal for her. Why would anyone go through the trouble to harass her? Getting out of bed, she walked into the living room. As she curled up on the couch, she grabbed the phone, dialing a number from memory.

"Hello?"

"Matt? It's Jackie. Are you busy?"

"No, just watching TV. What's up? I haven't heard from you in a while."

"I've been busy with Olympic Arena and the house."

"Yeah, I understand." Jackie could hear the skepticism in his voice.

"So, what's going on with you? How's your new commander working out?" she asked.

"Jackie, what's going on? We haven't talked in a few weeks. You don't just call me out of the blue to ask about work."

She sighed. "I . . . " Her voice caught in her throat, and she couldn't continue.

"Are you all right? What's wrong? What's happened?" Matt's voice rose in concern.

"I'm okay," she quickly assured him. She sniffed, reaching for a tissue. "I'm scared. That's all. Somebody's messing with me and I can't figure out why." She proceeded to outline the bizarre phone calls, letters, and packages she had been receiving. When she got to the break-in that night, Matt stopped her.

"Someone took the fuses out of your fuse box? Jackie, that's not right."

"The police think it's kids playing around."

"What do you think?"

"I don't know what to think."

"Jackie, it's okay to be scared. I would be. Hell, I'm scared for you. Is there someone you can stay with for a while?"

"I guess I could go to Kris's house."

"That's a good idea. Just be careful around Alex. From all the things you've told me, he doesn't sound quite right."

Jackie thought about the right way to answer. "He's okay really. I think their relationship is a little off. It's like they're putting on an act. But you're right. I don't think I want to be around them for any real length of time."

"Maybe you could stay on base."

"I'll look into it." Jackie's thoughts turned to Joel's invitation to stay at his place. Would that work? At least temporarily? If she could make it through this missile competition, she'd be able to concentrate on solving this mystery.

"You could always move," Matt offered.

"I'm not going to be scared into leaving. I'm not giving up my house."

Chapter 16

The next morning, Jackie called her parents. She didn't want to scare her mother by telling her about the break-in, but she needed to hear her reassuring voice.

"Jackie! How are things going? I've been thinking about you."

"I had a quick minute so thought I'd check in," Jackie said.

"What project are you working on?"

"Not a lot right now. I'm studying around the clock for Olympic Arena."

"Do you think that's such a good idea? I mean, it can't be healthy for you. Why don't you take a few days off?" her mom asked.

Jackie resisted the urge to laugh. "Mom, that's not how it works. This is a highly sought-after team; competition is fierce. Trust me, no one else is taking time off. Besides, it won't last forever."

"Sure, but when this is over you'll find something else to take up all your time. It's what you do, Jackie. You need to learn to relax."

Jackie had heard this speech before. She knew her mother was right. She waited patiently for her mother to continue.

"Maybe your dad and I could come for a visit. He has some vacation time coming up."

"Mom, now is not good. I don't have time to visit; maybe after the competition."

"Well, you let me know when. You know Dad will be on the road as soon as you give the word. He probably won't tell you, but he sure is proud of you. He'd do anything for you."

Jackie thought that was a stretch but had to admit he had a strange way of coming through for her when she needed him. When she was in college, her car was towed, and she didn't have a hundred dollars to get it back. It almost killed her, but she called her dad to ask him for a loan—only until her next paycheck. Within three hours he was standing on her doorstep with the money.

He had taken Jackie out for dinner, slipping her another twenty dollars "just because," then drove the three hours home. Jackie had never forgotten that. It was so unlike the cold, unfeeling father she'd grown up with. She stopped to wonder if this was why she put up with so much from the guys she dated . . . she was eternally hopeful that they would come through for her when she needed them the most.

"I promise, Mom. We'll set up something after the competition. Maybe we can meet somewhere halfway between here and there."

∼

After another sleepless night with multiple harassing phone calls, Jackie made up her mind. When she caught up with Joel outside the briefing room Monday morning, she pulled him aside. "Joel, did you mean it when you said I could crash at your house for a while?"

"Sure I did. Why? What's happened?"

"I simply need some rest. The phone calls are freaking me out, and I want to unwind. Will this be awkward for you?"

"No, of course not," he said as a smile crept over his face.

"This needs to be totally platonic. You do have an extra room, don't you?" Jackie clarified.

"You'll be safe with me," he reassured her. "Come by after work and I'll give you a key. Do you want me to go by your house with you to pick up your things?"

"No, I'll go by there right after work. They're letting us go at nineteen-thirty. How about if I pick up dinner too?" Jackie offered.

"Sounds great."

That evening, Joel opened a bottle of wine to go with the Chinese food Jackie brought over. Joel told stories of when he went through missile training, including the tricks the commanders played on him during his first alert.

Jackie laughed, sympathizing with him. She hadn't fallen for those same tricks, but only because she'd been forewarned.

As Jackie settled into the guest room that night, she was glad she'd decided to stay with Joel. He was a really nice guy. As she turned off the light, she thought once again that it was a shame there were no sparks between them.

Olympic Arena was only three nights away. Tension was high around the operations building. Jackie and her crew partner started and ended their day in the trainer with eight hours of study time in between.

When Jackie finally made it back to Joel's house, it was almost midnight. She was relieved to see that Joel had already gone to bed but had left a light on for her. She quietly made her way to her room, closing the door. Half asleep already, she didn't bother turning on the lights as she undressed, slipped under the covers wearing only her t-shirt and underwear and dropped off to sleep.

At first, Jackie wasn't sure what was happening. She felt a hand on her shoulder but was sure she must be dreaming. As the hand gently caressed her shoulder and then slid down her bare arm, she came awake, convinced that the intruder had somehow broken into Joel's house.

She rolled away, getting tangled in the sheets as she tried to get out of the bed.

"Shhh. It's me." Joel's voice broke through her panic. He reached out to stroke her hair.

"Get out of here! What are you doing?" Jackie tried to control her voice as she slapped his hand away.

Joel slid closer to her, pressing his body against hers, trapping her underneath him.

Jackie tried to scream, but his mouth closed over hers. She continued to fight him off, pushing at his chest and twisting her head to the side. "Get off!"

Joel suddenly released her. In her struggle, the sheets became free, and she fell out of the bed. Without bothering to get to her feet, she shuffled to the corner, grabbing the lamp off the bedside table as she went.

Joel sat up in the bed and looked at her. "What's wrong with you?"

"With me?!" Jackie was bordering on hysterics. "What are you doing?"

"I thought you liked me. I thought that's why you're staying here."

Jackie's mind raced. "Get out!"

"I'm sorry I scared you. I didn't mean to."

"What did you think would happen when you crept in here? I told you I was staying as a friend."

"We've been going out for weeks now. I didn't think you would mind."

"Wouldn't mind you forcing yourself on me? Wouldn't mind you scaring me to death?" she asked incredulously.

"I thought you might like the company. I know you've been lonely living by yourself."

"I'm not lonely. I like being alone." Jackie tried to control her racing heart.

"I'm sorry. I'll leave."

"No, I'll leave." Jackie pulled herself to her feet.

"Don't be ridiculous. It's two in the morning. I'll go back to my room. You can lock the door. Put the chair in front of it if you want to. I have an alert tomorrow, so I'll be gone before you get up. You won't even have to see me." Joel walked toward the door. As he closed the door, he said, "I really am sorry."

Jackie slid down the wall and sat in the dark, trying to decide what to do. Suddenly she was very tired again. Pulling herself up, she walked to the door. Locking it, she headed back to the bed. On second thought, she found the chair on the other side of the room and picked it up. It fit nicely under the handle as she jammed it securely in place. Then she stumbled back into bed, curling into a tight ball under the covers. A shudder ran through her as she willed herself to sleep.

True to his word, Joel was gone when Jackie left her room Wednesday morning. Jackie gathered her bag and loaded it in her car. As she drove away, she berated herself for being so stupid.

When she got back to her own house, Jackie showered and changed. She checked her answering machine and noted that she didn't have any hang-ups. She couldn't remember the last time she'd gone two nights in a row without hang-ups. Maybe the creep had given up.

With no more time to waste to get to work, Jackie pulled her front door closed behind her, double-checking the lock was secure.

∼

Captain Anderson was in rare form in the training room. He was digging through regulations, making hasty notes. Blakely was waiting for Jackie when she walked in. "You look like hell," he said.

"Nice to see you, too." Jackie tried to smile. "Come on. We have work to do."

The crew partners spent the next several hours reviewing notes and walking through wiring diagrams for the capsule, trying to foresee any and all scenarios. The what-if games were endless.

By lunchtime, Jackie was falling asleep in her books. "What's going on with you?" Blakely asked.

"Nothing I want to discuss. I didn't sleep well."

"It's almost over," he commented.

"I hope so," Jackie said, knowing they were talking about two different things.

That night, Jackie packed her bags for the trip to Vandenberg Air Force Base. The flight to California was due to leave from Whiteman the next morning at six. As she checked and rechecked her uniforms, Jackie started to get nervous about the competition.

There were only a handful of women in the missile career field and a rare few made it to Olympic Arena. She knew this competition was about more than her performance. People saw her as the representative of women trying to succeed in the Air Force. Her triumphs would be theirs to share. However, her failings would be magnified, blamed solely on the fact that she was female.

Chapter 17

He saw her get out of her car. She was good-looking, well-dressed. Not a bad body. Could use a little more in the chest and a little less in the backside, but no one was perfect, so they say.

"Excuse me." He caught her attention as she walked up the sidewalk toward the building. "I'm new around here and was wondering if you could recommend a good place to eat lunch."

She smiled a little warily. "I'm fairly new myself, but there's a diner around the corner on High Street. They have good soup."

"So is that where you take your lunch breaks?" he asked flirtatiously. *No wedding ring,* he noted.

She couldn't help but smile back. "Sometimes."

"I'll give it a try. And hopefully I'll run into you . . . in the near future."

She shrugged playfully. "Maybe." She smiled and tossed her hair over one shoulder as she hurried to work.

He watched her go, already planning their next encounter.

Chapter 18

When the taxi dropped Jackie off Saturday afternoon, her sense of relief at being home was tangible. She looked forward to sleeping for three days straight after the whirlwind trip to California that had been one challenge after the other.

The missiliers had competed on the second day, but their scores weren't posted until the third and final day. Waiting for the score posting was hell. She tortured herself—and Captain Blakely—about all the things they might have done wrong.

When the scores were finally posted, she was crushed. Although they had scored 276 out of 300, her crew had missed the number-one slot by four points. Jackie couldn't simply enjoy being second out of twenty-four crews. She was stuck replaying what she should have done differently. One clock reset, and they would have taken home the first-place crew trophy. The only crew with a higher score was also from Whiteman, so together the 351st Missile Wing had taken first place for the Operations Team. The wing commander had been very proud.

When Jackie walked up the sidewalk to her front door she saw the writing. The chalk numbers took on a familiar pattern as Jackie studied them. They were the operations' scores from Olympic Arena, starting from the lowest score closest to the street and ending with her score in large, bold, colorful chalk near her porch. The stars and exclamation points drawn around the number "276" were meant to make her feel good, but they only served as another reminder that Jackie was not quite good enough. The "281" written in smaller lettering above stabbed her pride. She stepped over the chalk markings and went into the house.

After Jackie finished her shower, she pulled on her favorite baggy sweatsuit and curled up on the couch. She had just clicked on the TV when the doorbell rang. Reluctantly she muted her show and walked to the door. She peered through the window to see a grinning Joel.

Jackie opened the front door, keeping the screen door latched.

"Great job, Jackie. I'm so proud of you!"

"Thanks, Joel. I take it the chalk art is yours?"

"I hope you don't mind. I wanted everyone to know how well you did." Joel was obviously pleased with his idea.

Jackie kept silent. She still wasn't comfortable around Joel and was too tired to deal with him.

"Do you want to catch a movie?"

Jackie sighed. "I just want to relax for a while."

"That's okay. I can do that."

"Joel, I don't think it would be a good idea for us to go out anymore."

Joel froze. "If this is about the night at my house, I said I was sorry. It won't happen again."

"It's not only that. I'm not interested in having a relationship right now," she lied, trying to spare his feelings.

"Right," Joel said sarcastically. "The old 'let's be friends' routine. Got it. Have a nice day." Joel was off the porch before Jackie had a chance to say anything else.

Feeling slightly guilty, she couldn't help but think, *Probably for the best.* She didn't know what else she could say. Locking the front door, she went back to the TV.

Jackie was looking forward to getting to bed early. She pulled out her favorite sleepshirt. The phone rang. Not this *again*, she thought. After a slight hesitation, she picked up the receiver. "Hello?"

"Jackie, this is Daniel. Welcome home."

Warmth filled her body. "Thanks. What have you been up to?"

"Busy watching score postings. I know you're disappointed at not being first, but you did a great job."

"How did you know I was disappointed?"

"It was all over your face. It was televised, remember? They zoomed in on the Whiteman team right after they posted your score. You looked pretty pissed."

"That's one way to put it," she admitted.

"At least it's over. Do you want to go to Kansas City to celebrate? There's this jazz club I've been wanting to try out."

Her heart raced. She was exhausted but excited to see Daniel again. Then a thought occurred to her. "Would this be considered a date?"

Daniel laughed. "Yes, I think you could call it a date. Why?"

"Aren't you my counselor? Are we allowed to date?"

Daniel considered the question. "Olympic Arena is over and the pressure from the competition was why you were sent to me. I declare you cured. Now can we go?"

"Give me an hour." As soon as the receiver was in the cradle, Jackie flew into action, pulling items from her closet, trying to decide what you were supposed to wear on a date to a jazz club with your former counselor.

~

Kris and Jackie stopped to admire the beautiful flowers planted along the walk in the park. This track was the most scenic in the area and the most accessible. Jackie had missed these walks with Kris. It was nice to have time to do what she wanted for a change.

"Joel stopped by the other day," Kris offered. "He's pretty broken up that you don't want to go out with him."

"I told you before that there were no sparks. The little stunt he pulled at his house cinched it."

"I understand and don't blame you. Why didn't you stay with me anyway? You're always welcome at our place."

"I know. I made a bad choice."

"So are you officially dating Daniel now?" Kris absently plucked a leaf from a nearby tree.

"I'm not sure what makes it official, but I've been seeing a lot of him these last few days. What do you think of him?"

"Seems nice enough. Why don't you two come over this weekend for dinner, and we can get to know him better?"

Jackie agreed.

"Louis is still pining for you, you know," Kris said.

Jackie sighed. "There was never a chance there."

"How do you do it? How do you get all these guys falling all over you?"

"I'm not doing anything," Jackie protested. "I'm not even looking for anything."

"That must be the secret."

"What about you and Alex?"

"What about us?"

"How are you getting along?" Jackie asked gently.

Kris shrugged. "Same as always."

"If you don't mind me saying, I never understood how you ended up together. He doesn't seem like your type."

Kris was silent for a few minutes, and Jackie let her drift with her thoughts.

Finally, Kris spoke. "I was always a little wild in high school."

"No!" Jackie declared in mock shock.

That made Kris smile. "When it was time to settle down, I thought I needed someone who could tame that wild side of me."

"And now what do you think?"

"I miss my wild side," Kris admitted.

◈

D inner was magnificent, Kris," Daniel commented. "I'd love the recipe."

"You cook?" Kris and Jackie asked at the same time, eliciting a laugh from both men.

"Yes, I can cook," Daniel answered with a grin. "And I clean up after myself too."

Jackie saw Alex scowl slightly as Kris laughed.

After dinner, Kris and Jackie cleared the table while Alex and Daniel made their way to where the new garage was to be built.

"Daniel's a nice guy," Kris said, handing Jackie the plates covered with the remains of blueberry pie.

Jackie's smile was hard to hide. "He is something."

Kris held on to the last plate as Jackie tried to take it from her. Jackie looked up to meet her eyes. Kris started laughing and let it go. "I can't wait to hear what Alison has to say about this new development."

"She might try to steal him away if I'm not careful."

Jackie finished loading the dishwasher and added the soap. "Louis stopped me at the club the other day," Jackie said.

"What did he want?" Kris placed the pots and pans in the soapy water to soak.

"He was trying to act normal, but I could tell he was self-conscious about something. He had trouble meeting my eyes."

Kris nodded. "I think you're right. He's probably the one that left you the globe. Did he mention it?"

"No way! I'm glad he didn't actually. I don't know what to say to him. He's not my type." Jackie thought for a moment as she wiped off the counter. "He seemed to get serious so fast. From lunch at the club to 'I'd give you the world.' That's enough to scare anyone away."

"I don't think he meant any harm. He's in love."

Jackie barked a laugh. "How can he fall in love with someone like me? I didn't do anything special."

"Men like him have another side to them. He may surprise you."

"Oh, ye who is so wise in the ways of men," Jackie teased. "What is it I should be looking for in the man of my dreams?"

Kris snapped a towel at her. "You scoff, but men don't show all their cards at once. They all hold something back for that special someone."

"And am I supposed to be holding something back too?"

"You do!" Kris insisted. "You haven't let your guard down for anyone. Not even this Daniel guy. So far, he's just a play toy for you."

"Not a bad game so far."

Chapter 19

The following week, Jackie found herself wandering around the weight room on base. Maybe a few more sets wouldn't hurt. After another half hour, she knew that she was stalling the inevitable. She needed to go home. Although Olympic Arena was over and her schedule was becoming more routine, the hang-ups kept coming. Jackie couldn't believe this jerk wouldn't give up. It had to be getting boring for him too.

The house was dark when she pulled in. The sun had set, and the porch was filled with shadows. The ivy growing on the trellis now seemed like a hindrance rather than a decorative touch. Walking onto the porch, she opened the screen door. She tried the handle to the front door and it was locked. Well, that was a good sign. Turning the key in the lock, she pushed the door open and reached inside to turn on the lights. Lights worked—another good sign.

After securing the bolt behind her, she picked up a pair of scissors and proceeded to make a thorough search of the house. After convincing herself that all was well, Jackie went into the kitchen to make dinner.

Putting a pot of water on the stove to boil, she picked up the phone to call her sister.

"So, Daniel seems to be a regular around your place these days," Alison prompted after the usual chit chat. "Is there something you should be telling me?"

"Not like I could hide anything from you." Jackie smiled. "It wouldn't do me any good. You'd get your information from Kris."

"Well, there is that, but I'd rather hear it firsthand." Alison's teasing tone changed to one of concern. "What about your phone calls and letters? Any insight?"

"No. I finally got around to taking the letters to the police station. They made copies but said they really can't do much about it because sending letters isn't against the law. The writer hasn't threatened me or anything."

"So they're going to wait for him to attack you before they take this seriously?" The pitch in Alison's voice rose. "This is why more attacks aren't prevented."

"They did ask me about the guys named in the letter and anyone else I thought might want to scare me."

"Did you tell them about your night at Joel's?"

"That's something I would rather forget. I was stupid. I didn't give them details, but I did tell them that I went out with him a few times and that he was upset when I said I didn't want to see him anymore." Jackie added, "Now he ignores me in the squadron. He even walks the other way when he sees me coming."

"He's immature. He's so good-looking that he probably expects women to fall at his feet."

Jackie thought about that. She had to agree. "Maybe I'm overreacting. I'm not used to so much attention from guys. Maybe this is normal courting for someone."

"Jackie, there isn't anything normal about whoever is doing this. Watch out for yourself."

❧

Kris looked across the table at Louis. He was such a nice guy. She knew that sounded like a cliché, but she didn't know how else to put it. He was smart, good-looking with red hair and blue eyes. He even looked sharp in uniform. If she had to name a fault, it would be that he tried too hard.

"So have you talked to Jackie lately?" he asked, trying to sound casual as he cut into his lunch.

"She stopped into the office before she went on alert." Kris took a bite of her sandwich.

"How's she doing? I hear she's had some trouble at her house."

"You did?" replied Kris, mildly surprised. Louis seemed to know a lot about what went on with the people on base. "She's doing okay. Personally, I don't think she's taking it seriously enough."

"It's kind of creepy." Louis chewed slowly. After a sip of water, he added, "Make sure to tell her she can call me if she needs anything."

"I'll let her know. I'm sure she'll appreciate the support." Kris looked closely at him. "Louis, what is it about Jackie?"

"What do you mean?"

"When was the last time you went on a date—not with Jackie?"

Louis thought about it.

"That's what I mean," Kris said. "You're hooked on her, but she hasn't given you much hope, has she?"

"She'll come around. She has too many other things going on right now. I can wait until she's ready. Then I'll be there."

"What if she's never ready, Louis?" Kris hated doing this to him, but she didn't want to see him hurt either.

"I'm not worried about it, Kris. You shouldn't be either."

Jackie, we need to talk." Joel's voice sounded tinny through the phone line.

Jackie glanced at the clock. She wasn't pleased with the intrusion of the phone into her slumber. "What do we need to talk about, Joel? What could you possibly have to say to me so early in the morning?"

"The cops were at my house last night."

Jackie was surprised. "Why?"

"They were asking about you. They asked if I had been bothering you." Jackie could hear the tension in his voice. "What did you tell them?"

Jackie hesitated. She hadn't expected the police to go to his house. "They asked me who I had gone out with recently, that's all. I'm sure they're asking other people questions too," although Jackie doubted this was true.

"What's going on?" Joel sounded increasingly irritated. "What's happened that would send you to the police?"

"I'm tired of the phone calls. After the incident with my fuses being pulled, the cops asked if anything else strange had been happening."

"And? What else haven't you told me?"

Now Jackie was starting to get agitated. "I don't report to you!"

Joel was quiet for a moment. "I'm sorry." Joel's voice was calmer, but he was still tense, on edge. "I mean, I care about you, and I want to know what else has happened to you that makes you worried enough to go to the police."

Jackie tried to steady her voice. No reason to get heated with Joel. "I told them about the letters I've been getting."

"So? What does that have to do with me?" The strain in Joel's voice was evident.

"Nothing directly. You were mentioned in one of the poems. The police asked for more information about each person named and I told them."

Suddenly Joel was angry again. "Great! Now I'll be constantly looking over my shoulder to see if I'm being followed."

"Why would you have to do that? If you haven't done anything wrong, there's no reason for the police to talk to you again. What do you have to hide?" Something in his tone was not sitting right with her. He was blowing this way out of proportion.

"I haven't done anything wrong! The police were still at my door. And the neighbors saw them. They'll be asking questions."

Why was he getting so bent out of shape? Suddenly something clicked in Jackie's head. She decided to play a hunch. "You don't have anything to worry about. The police have the letters, and they're going to fingerprint them. We'll know soon enough who it is, and then you'll be off the hook."

Silence.

"Joel?"

"Jackie, we need to talk. Can I come over?" His voice was humble now.

"What do you have to say?"

"I want to see you in person."

"Anything you have to say to me can be said over the phone."

"Please let me come over and explain." Joel was practically begging now.

"Joel, did you write the letters?"

"Can I come over?" Jackie heard the desperation in his voice.

"Did you write the letters?" Jackie persisted.

"Jackie, let me come over and see you."

"Stay away from me. Do you hear?" Jackie was calm but firm. "Stay away from me and my house. I don't want you anywhere near me." Things were starting to make sense.

"But, Jackie, I didn't mean—"

"I don't care what you meant. You stay away from me." Her control almost slipped as her voice began to rise.

"Are you going to tell the squadron commander?" Joel was pleading now. Jackie almost felt sorry for him.

Then she thought about all the sleepless nights she had been through lately and anger surged in her. But then it was like hitting a brick wall when she envisioned the trouble that was yet to come if the guys in the squadron found out that she "couldn't take a joke." This would be as hard, if not harder, on her and her career than it would be for Joel.

"If you stay away from me, I won't go to the commander, but you had better keep your distance."

Chapter 20

Joel was furious. "That bitch!" he yelled, throwing the phone against the wall of his apartment. He stood with his hands on his hips, fuming. His fury prevented him from focusing. The sight of cops knocking on his door kept running over and over in his mind. "How dare she try to embarrass me in front of my neighbors!" he said, though no one was there to hear him.

Joel ran his hand through his hair in frustration. His eyes caught a photo frame lying face down on the tile near where the broken phone had landed. Rushing to pick it up, he turned it over gently. Shards of glass ripped the photo of a young boy and a middle-aged woman underneath.

Kneeling, he tried to pull the glass away from the photo without doing further damage. Blood welled on the tip of his middle finger. He sucked the redness away, thinking of his mother.

He wondered if she had put Jackie up to this. It was something she would do. His mother was always trying to teach him a lesson, or so she said. This was his fault for being born. His mother reminded him of that over and over.

Joel had tried so hard to please her and to stay out of her way when she was in one of her moods.

He learned quickly to fend for himself, mastering the use of the microwave at a young age—something he had to learn when she didn't come home until well after bedtime. To this day, he still couldn't stand the smell of popcorn.

She had worn dresses that he thought were too short for a mother and painted her eyes so they looked too large for her face. Sometimes she wasn't alone when she stumbled through the door. Whenever Joel heard the sound of a man's voice, he'd hide under the covers. No one ever came into his room though.

About the time Joel was eleven, his mother had started getting sick a lot, throwing up almost every day. She was grumpier than usual, swearing constantly.

That's when his own problems started.

He tried to hide it as long as he could, but his clothes had started to stink. Joel didn't know how to work the washing machine, and when he tried to wash out his wet underwear in the bathroom, his mother yelled at him for leaving his clothes laying about.

His teacher finally sent a note home to his mother.

She flew into a rage, accusing him of doing it on purpose to make her life harder than it was. After a few weeks of punishment, ranging from extra chores to sleeping in a diaper, she finally took him to the doctor.

The doctor had said the bedwetting wasn't his fault, but his mother hadn't cared. She said only a selfish baby would put her through this, and she didn't have time for another baby.

The next morning, his mother wasn't home when Joel got up. He stripped his sheets, piling them on the washer the way she told him to. He went to school and returned. She still wasn't home when it was time for dinner, so Joel opened a can of soup.

Hearing the key in the lock, he had pulled out another bowl for his mother. When he turned to look at her, he was shocked at how horrible she looked. Her sunken eyes and stringy hair were a far cry from the way she usually looked when she went out.

He had been scared, but she pushed him away when he tried to find out what was wrong. She had gone straight to bed.

She stayed there the whole next day, refusing to eat even when Joel brought her food. She cried and slept. After the third day of this, he got scared, gathering enough courage to go to the nice old lady next door who always smiled at him when he got off the bus. He was sure she would help.

When Joel knocked at her door, her eyes were bright with the pleasure of seeing him. Then the light faded as he tried to explain what was going on with his mother.

Leaving him sitting at her kitchen table with a piece of apple pie and ice cream, the nice lady went to Joel's house.

He never knew what she did to make his mother feel better. When he went home, his mother had taken a shower and was sitting on the couch.

She didn't look at him but got up and went into the kitchen. Scrambling some eggs, she told him to get to the table. Although he wasn't hungry, he cleaned his plate. When he got up the nerve to ask her if she was feeling better, she only said that one baby was enough.

It was years later before he understood his mother's words. He still felt sick when he thought about his brother or sister that never was, just because he couldn't control his bladder.

In his apartment, fifteen years later, Joel broke into a sweat thinking about it. He hated that his mother could still make his life miserable. And now Jackie was doing the same thing to him!

He treated her well. Opened his home to her. Gave her whatever she needed. And this is how she repaid him—cops at his door!

At the thought, Joel's rage intensified. Turning rapidly, he punched the wall nearest him. The jagged hole in the living room wall was a visual reminder that his emotions were becoming more difficult to control.

Chapter 21

After breakfast, Jackie threw herself into her restoration project. It was time to get her life in order, and she would begin by completing her bedroom.

As she surveyed the house, she was pleased with how it was turning out. Her living room and dining room were almost complete. She needed carpeting but didn't want to put it down while she was still tearing out plaster from the walls and ceilings in other rooms. Her bedroom awaited fresh paint, and curtains for the French doors would provide privacy from the living room.

Pulling out the measuring tape, she began to calculate how much fabric she would need to buy. Glancing out the window, she saw a car drive slowly past. She didn't think much about it until she saw another car that looked very similar drive by less than five minutes later.

Jackie put down her notes, walking to the living room window. She peered out from behind the curtains and waited. Sure enough, the same car was coming around the corner again.

Jackie stepped out onto the porch. The driver sped off, but she was pretty sure she recognized Louis behind the wheel.

That makes no sense, she thought. *He doesn't live around here.*

Jackie moved back into the house, making a mental note to talk to Kris about it. Maybe she knew why Louis would be driving by her house but not stopping. She would have thought if he really wanted to talk to her, he would have knocked on the door.

For now, she had other things to think about. As she finished her measuring, she thought about the next day's alert. She'd been paired with the Alpha Flight Commander, whom she heard was hard to work for because he was such a perfectionist. She was looking forward to the challenge.

$\sim$

Two days later, Jackie ran into her competition crew commander. "I heard last night's alert went well," Captain Blakely commented when he saw Jackie coming out of the codes vault.

"How did you hear that already? We just got back," Jackie said, shifting her technical order case from one hand to the other. The bulky, black bag was weighted down with books.

"I have my sources. You'd make a good Deputy Flight Commander. You sure did well for me during OA."

"So that's what this crew pairing was about! When will they tell me if I've been selected?" Jackie was excited. It hadn't crossed her mind that the deputy position in Alpha Flight was coming open.

"Probably pretty soon. The Alpha commander just has to give his feedback to the squadron commander." Blakely looked past Jackie and waved. "There's Joel. We need to pick up codes. We're going out to Juliet today."

"Why are you still here?" she asked. "Shouldn't you have left already?" The Juliet Launch Control Center was two and a half hours from the Air Force base.

"We're taking the helicopter and there was a delay. We should be leaving within the half-hour."

Joel walked past Jackie and Blakely without saying a word. Raising his eyebrows, Blakely looked at Jackie. She shrugged.

Blakely said, "Let me know if you hear anything before I do."

"I will. Have a good alert." Jackie continued down the hall, adjusting the TO bag again.

Chapter 22

Police Captain Mike Shuster looked around the squad room. These were the finest detectives and police officers working for the city of Lee Summit. Surely working together, they could get a break in this investigation.

Shuster cleared his throat to get everyone's attention. A few officers in the back of the room moved forward to grab a seat. Shuster's partner, Ashton Mills, handed him a cup of coffee and sat down in the first row.

"Let's start from the beginning. What do we know about Tammy Middleton?" Shuster asked.

Officer Mark Talley, sitting in the front row, began. "She was twenty-nine, single, five-foot-six, athletic build." He checked his notes. "She lived alone; moved into her house about one year ago."

The officer sitting next to him chimed in. "She worked at the Bank of Lee Summit on South Main Street as a bank manager. Her coworkers believe she had a boyfriend, but Middleton didn't talk about her personal life at work."

Mills turned to face Officer Adam Hunter. "What makes them think there was a boyfriend?"

"Women's intuition mostly."

A few of the officers laughed, but Shuster was not so dismissive. "Believe it or not, guys, there's something to intuition when it comes to romance. What specifically did they say?"

"The way she would come back from lunch with a smile on her face. Said she changed her hair and makeup. Nothing concrete," Hunter explained.

"Have we checked her phone records to see if we can locate this boyfriend?"

"We haven't gotten the records from the phone company yet. Supposed to have them today," answered Mills.

"What else? Hobbies? Interests?"

Talley said, "She belonged to the local gym but didn't go regularly. They've provided their membership list, and we're going over it. There was a sewing machine in her home and tools in the garage. Fresh paint in a few rooms, but no cans of paint leftover so we don't know if she did it herself or hired it out."

"Go over her receipts, bank book—anything that might show if she paid someone else to do it. What about the neighbors?" Shuster asked.

This time Hunter referred to his notes. "The neighbor closest to Middleton was away visiting family in Texas for a week prior. He got back yesterday. Didn't know anything helpful. The neighbor on the other side is a single guy who plays drums in a band. The night Middleton was killed, he was on stage at the Double Crown Lounge on Green Street. We've already confirmed he was there all night."

"Across the street is an empty field," Hunter added. "Patrolmen canvassed the whole neighborhood. No one saw or suspected anything."

"Did you ask about a boyfriend?"

A patrolman in the back row spoke up. "We asked about regulars coming and going from the house, but no one mentioned a boyfriend."

Shuster was frustrated. "What does her family say?"

"Parents said they got a regular phone call from her every weekend, but mostly they just talked about work," Talley said. "Her brother hasn't talked to her in a few months but apparently that's not unusual. He lives in Idaho with his wife and three children. Says he and his sister didn't have much in common."

Shuster asked, "What did we get back from forensics?"

"Cause of death was blunt force trauma to the back of the head," Mills said. "Wound matches a baseball bat we found on the scene. Only Middleton's prints. She also had a few broken ribs, probably from the same bat. No unexpected DNA anywhere. Looks like whoever it was wore gloves and was careful not to get too close."

"The house was in disarray as if there were a scuffle throughout a number of rooms." Talley got up and pointed to the photos posted to the board. "End table knocked over in the living room, broken lamp on the floor, rugs out of place. In the kitchen, the table looked as if it had been shoved aside and some of the chairs were tipped over. The final assault was made in the office area. Looks like Middleton was trying to make it out."

"Okay, folks, it's been two days. Mills, get those phone records and pull the bank records as well. Talley, re-interview the neighbors and Middleton's coworkers. If intuition is all we have, let's try to make it more concrete. You need to ask the right questions. People see more than they realize. Focus on the boyfriend or an old boyfriend. She's lived here a year. Someone must know her."

Chapter 23

Grabbing his drink, he slid open the patio door. He walked out to the railing and examined the backyard. He loved it out here. It was so quiet and peaceful. The pine boughs swayed gently in the wind along his back-property line. He listened to the songs of the birds and the chattering of squirrels. Leaves crackled as they wrestled in the underbrush. He smiled and sauntered back to his favorite patio chair. Sinking into the seat, he took a swig from his glass and contemplated his latest challenge.

The man was pleased. She was special somehow. Things would be different this time. She was insecure in so many areas, it should be easy to mold her the way he wanted.

Setting the glass down on the decking, he reached into the side pocket of his chair. His fingers closed around the familiar wood handle. He caressed it with his thumb as he brought the slingshot onto his lap. With his other hand, he reached down to the small stack of stones that sat next to his chair. Carefully fitting a stone into the sling, he pulled it back slowly, testing the strength of the rubber bands. Satisfied, he carefully took aim.

With a thwack from the bands, the stone flew, bouncing off a tree trunk at the back of the yard with a crack. *Not a bad shot,* he thought, *but I used to be better.* He picked up another stone and cradled it in the leather. This time he stood to aim.

The shot met its mark with a dull thud. Smiling, he walked into the yard. Now that was better.

The man used to be dead-on with the slingshot—his weapon of choice. He had tried a BB-gun but hadn't found it challenging enough. The slingshot was an old weapon, one not many people bothered to master. By seven years old, he could beat anyone in the neighborhood. He set up targets in the woods behind his house and spent hours pretending to be a great hunter.

He was mastering his double shot when his sister ratted him out. She must have been watching from the upstairs window because he had no idea she had seen him. Before dinner that night, his father had summoned him to the study. Encounters with his father were never pleasant. He listened as his father ranted and berated him. The tirade had ended with a severe beating as his father used a leather strap to teach him "not to be cruel to animals."

All of that over a few squirrels and a half dozen birds. His contempt for his father remained fresh. His father had no appreciation for how difficult it was to hit a moving target. He'd always demanded that the young boy stand still for his beating.

Breaking free from his musing, he stuck the slingshot in his back pocket and bent over to pick up the squirrel by its tail as it still twitched slightly. He carried his kill into the tree line and tossed it on the growing pile of carcasses. He wiped his hands together dismissively, walking back to the house to refill his drink.

Chapter 24

When Jackie got home she roamed through the house trying to decide what to do next. The phone rang. "Hello," Jackie answered brightly.

"Hello, yourself stranger. Been keeping odd hours again, I see," Daniel said.

"Yes, I can't help myself. There are so many men, so little time." Jackie enjoyed the way she was able to banter with Daniel. He seemed so self-assured but not conceited.

"How did the alert go?"

"It was slow. A little maintenance at a few sites but nothing to keep me up all night. What about you?"

"A few nervous breakdowns, a social disorder or two, and a few other odds and ends—none of them mine though, so you're safe." Jackie could hear him smiling and pictured him leaning back in his office chair.

"Well, maybe you deserve a break from the drudgery. Do you want to catch up over dinner tonight?" Jackie asked.

"I have plans tonight with an old friend, but maybe tomorrow . . . ?" Daniel replied with hope in his voice.

"Sure, we can make it tomorrow." Jackie wondered about this "old friend," but didn't want to appear clingy. "How about we meet at Logan's Steakhouse, say, nineteen-hundred?"

"Sounds good. I'll see you there."

Jackie hung up the phone, heading toward the bathroom. She'd already tiled the area around the tub and installed an old-fashioned shower that ran on the outside of the wall but needed to decide what to do with the rest of the room. As she tried to concentrate, her thoughts kept returning to Daniel's old friend.

Was it a he or a she? Why did it matter to her? She and Daniel were only friends, and here she was feeling jealous. They hadn't even kissed good night.

"Focus, Jackie, focus," she told herself. Then she realized she had gotten so distracted that she forgot to tell Daniel about Joel and the letters. She'd have to fill him in tomorrow night.

～

As Jackie double-checked the locks and turned off the lights, she thought she heard a sound on the side of the house. She listened closely but didn't hear anything else. She quickly finished up and crawled into bed, anxious to escape into the love story she was close to finishing.

As the handsome sailor confessed his love to the beautiful maiden, her mind drifted to Matt. Last she'd heard he was dating a civilian he'd met at a rock climbing club.

Outside, a gust of wind rustled the tree that covered the roof above her room. The noise unnerved her. The phone rang, causing Jackie to jump. "Stop being silly," she told herself.

"Hello?" Jackie answered, wondering who would be calling so late.

Nothing.

"No!" Jackie yelled as she slammed the phone down. This was supposed to be over! Joel wrote the letters. She had assumed he had been making the phone calls too. But he was on alert . . .

The phone rang again. *They do have phones in the capsules,* Jackie thought. The phone rang again. Jackie picked it up and let the receiver fall back into the cradle.

On instinct, she picked up the phone, dialing before it could ring again. She needed to talk to someone.

"Hello," a male voice answered.

"Hi, Matt. It's Jackie." Jackie wasn't sure Matt would even be interested in talking to her. It had been almost a month since they last spoke.

"What's wrong?" he asked. Jackie had to smile at Matt's insight.

"I'm a little spooked."

"Another call?"

"Two so far tonight."

Matt sighed. "You really should call the police."

"They'd probably think I'm crying wolf. They've already been here twice since I moved in."

"That's what they get paid for."

"Let's talk about something else," Jackie suggested. "Keep me company for a while." Matt and Jackie fell into an easy conversation built upon shared friends and missile experiences.

In the middle of Matt's story about his new crew partner, the phone suddenly went quiet. Jackie's bedside lamp continued to cast shadows on the ceiling. "Matt? Matt?!"

Oh my God. The line is dead, Jackie realized. "Don't panic. Don't panic," she told herself. "Yeah, right," Jackie argued aloud with herself. "That's what all those stupid females in the movies say right before the killer chops them to pieces."

Jackie slid out of bed, moving quickly to the telephone in the living room. It was dead too. Trying to remain calm, she went back to her bedroom and slipped on a pair of jeans. Just in case, she picked up the receiver at her bedside again. Still nothing.

Her heart was beating wildly. She tried to still her mind so she could concentrate.

Heading to the front door, she grabbed her keys from the table. As quietly as she could, she unlocked the front door. Then, with a sudden rush of adrenaline, she pulled open the door, pushed through the screen, and ran onto the porch. Out of the corner of her eye, she spotted the three-foot iron rod she had been using to knock plaster from the ceiling. On instinct, she grabbed it and ran across the front yard toward her car. For such a small yard, it seemed to take forever.

The street was dark with no traffic and no street lights. Stepping into the road, Jackie's foot slipped, and she landed hard on her left side. With the hair standing up on the nape of her neck, she pushed herself from the ground. As she fumbled with the car keys, she imagined a pursuer hot on her heels.

Finally, she unlocked the car, climbed in, and locked the doors. The engine turned over on the first try, and Jackie slammed the accelerator to the floor without bothering to check for traffic.

As she drove fearfully through the streets of her Warrensburg neighborhood, Jackie tried to hold back the tears. She needed to find a phone. At the first major intersection, she pulled into a 7-Eleven that was open all night.

When she stepped from the car, Jackie realized she didn't have shoes on. She was only wearing her jeans and a tank top. At this point, she didn't care. She rushed into the store, still fighting the panic. "I need to use your phone."

The man behind the counter saw her wild eyes and didn't even question her. He handed the phone across the counter and watched as she dialed 911.

"Nine-one-one. What's your emergency?"

"I'm not sure. I mean, I'm Jackie Austin. I live at two-oh-six West North Street. I think someone is . . . I don't know. I was on the phone, and the phone went dead." Jackie finally began to cry.

"Miss Austin, please stay on the line. I'm sending someone to your house right now. They will be there in a minute. Are you okay?" the operator asked.

"I'm okay. Just scared."

"Miss Austin, the police officers are at your house. Will you open the door for them?"

"I'm not there. I'm at a store. The phone was dead."

"Can you go back to your house and meet them?"

"I don't want to go back there."

"It's okay. The police are there now. There's no one else. Can you make it back?"

Jackie hesitated. She was so scared, but what else could she do? "Yes. I'll be there in a few minutes."

Jackie thanked the clerk and returned to her car.

When she got back to her house, two police cars were parked on the street with lights flashing. Three officers were standing in her front yard talking. She felt foolish now. All this for a disconnected phone line? What was she thinking?

Some of her neighbors were standing on their porches watching the scene.

"Miss Austin?" One of the officers approached her as she got out of the car. "I'm Officer Dixon. Are you all right?"

"I'll be okay. I feel silly. I guess I got spooked when the phone went dead."

"Can we go inside and look around?" the officer asked.

"Of course." Jackie led the way through the yard. The front door was still open from her quick getaway. Jackie flipped on the light in the living room and stopped inside the door, afraid to go any farther. Officer Dixon walked around Jackie to the phone on the table. He picked it up. "There seems to be a dial tone now."

"Honest! The phone cut off in the middle of our conversation, and then I couldn't get a dial tone," Jackie insisted.

"We believe you, Miss Austin," the officer assured her. "As a matter of fact, about the same time you were calling nine-one-one, we received another frantic phone call from someone in Montana insisting that we check on you because your phone went dead."

Jackie was touched. "I should've called Matt back from the store to tell him I was all right."

"Do you have other phones in the house?"

Jackie led him into her room to check that phone too. It had a dial tone.

"Miss Austin, let's look around the rest of your house to make sure everything's locked up. The other officers are checking the outside."

Jackie and Officer Dixon went from room to room, but everything seemed to be in order. All the doors and windows were locked and nothing was missing.

"We'll keep a patrol car in the area and watch your house. Will you be okay here or do you want to stay somewhere else?"

Jackie thought of the last time she decided to stay somewhere else. "No, I'll be fine here. Maybe I was overreacting."

"Don't worry about that. It's better to be safe than sorry. We'll be here if you need us," Officer Dixon said as he headed to the front door.

Locking the door behind the policeman, Jackie went back to her room. She called Matt and, after thanking him for calling the police, filled him in on everything since their phone conversation was cut off. Matt was relieved that the police were watching, but wanted Jackie to leave the house, at least for the night. Jackie thanked Matt again and promised to call him the next day.

Jackie didn't want to leave. She refused to give up. Her dad had told her it was a mistake to buy this house. Was he right? What would he say when he heard about this? Would he think she was being overly dramatic, calling the police? Or would he say this was what she deserved—a young woman buying a house on her own?

She lay on the bed with her clothes on. On second thought, she got up and grabbed the pair of scissors she had with her sewing equipment. As she lay down again and turned off the light, she knew she was being silly. What kind of damage was she going to do with a pair of sewing scissors? She tried to rest her mind so she could sleep.

~

After an hour of staring at the ceiling, Jackie got up and put on her shoes. Stuffing a few items into a gym bag, she called Kris.

Jackie pulled in to the same 7-Eleven she'd stopped at a few hours ago. She wanted to say thanks to the person behind the counter and to let them know everything was all right. As she stepped out of her car, a police car pulled up behind her and rolled down his window. It was Officer Dixon.

"Is everything all right, Miss Austin?"

"Please call me Jackie," she replied. "Yes, everything's okay. I decided that it would be better if I went to my girlfriend's house for the night."

"Probably not a bad idea."

"I'm really sorry I troubled you with all this. So many bizarre things have been going on lately. I'm probably making a mountain out of a molehill."

"It's not your imagination, Miss—I mean, Jackie." Officer Dixon wiped a hand over his eyes, trying to decide how much to tell her. "The officers searched outside your house tonight. Near your cellar door on the side of your house, there's a box where the phone line comes in from the street. They found footprints there and fresh tool marks. Have you been working out there lately?"

Jackie's eyes widened. "No."

"It may be nothing. We're going to look again in the morning when there's more light. In the meantime, I think staying with your girlfriend is the right thing to do. Is there a number where we can reach you?"

Jackie recited the number while trying to grasp what the officer had told her. Someone was outside her house? While she was there? He could have caught her when she ran to the car. And when she fell! Jackie felt herself shaking.

Officer Dixon quickly got out of his car and put his arm around her shoulder to steady her. "It's going to be all right. I think he's trying to scare you. For what reason, I can't imagine. His idea of fun, I guess."

Jackie stood up straighter. "I'm all right. I think I need to get some sleep."

"I'll follow you to your friend's house. Does she know you're coming?"

Jackie nodded, "I called her before I left home. Can you wait while I go inside for a minute?" She walked into the 7-Eleven and spoke with the clerk. As she returned to her car, she waved at the policeman who waited for her patiently. It was reassuring to know he was there.

As she drove to Kris's house, she thought about how the bizarre events could be tied together. Joel wrote the letters, but he couldn't have made the calls. At least he couldn't have been the one that disconnected her phone last night. He had been on alert. Louis probably left the globe on her porch, but he was harmless, wasn't he? She wanted to believe it was all coincidence. The break-ins were kids like the police thought. Who else would go to all this trouble?

Chapter 25

The next few weeks were chaotic for Jackie. She changed her phone number, which stopped the calls for a while, but eventually they started up again with less frequency. She had trouble sleeping but was afraid to tell anyone at work for fear her ability to work would be called into question.

Anyone working with nuclear weapons was monitored through the Personnel Reliability Program. Any little thing could throw one's reliability to work with nuclear weapons into question—starting a new medicine, marital problems, or money problems. She had seen people pulled off alert for all kinds of things, and she didn't want to be one of them.

At least the letters had stopped.

The phone rang, causing Jackie to jump.

She picked it up in her bedroom. "Hello."

"Good morning!" Alison said cheerfully. "Taking the day off, I see."

Jackie relaxed, flopping down on her bed. "I had alert yesterday so I'm not due back in until tomorrow."

"I'm just checking in. I haven't heard from you in a few days," her sister said.

"Sorry. This new job is kicking my butt."

"I thought you wanted stan-eval."

Jackie had been selected for deputy flight commander, then was quickly chosen to be in the Standardization and

Evaluation Branch. "I do. It's a great job. But now, not only do I have to pull alerts, train, and study, I have to evaluate how the others are doing."

"Do people get mad at you for that?"

"For what? Telling them what they're doing wrong?" Jackie asked.

"Sure. No one likes being graded, do they?

Jackie thought about that for a minute. "I think it's how you tell them. Some evaluators are real assholes. That makes the rest of us look like nice guys."

"If you compare yourself to the worst of the bunch . . . "

"Actually most missiliers really want to be stan-eval eventually. We only pull two or three alerts a month instead of the normal eight because we need time to do everything else."

"So, how goes the dating scene?"

"Joel's avoiding me, which is fine with me."

"What about Louis? He seems like a nice guy."

"Nice, but a bit much," Jackie said. "He still says hi to me when I see him on base, but he doesn't ask me out anymore."

"And Daniel?" Her sister was not going to let up.

Jackie smiled. "He's a big flirt, not sure if there's more to him or not. He doesn't like to go anywhere—not local at least. He thinks nothing about driving an hour to Kansas City for dinner but won't go to a place here in town."

"That's a little strange," Alison said.

"I've decided men in general are a little strange. What about you? How's Lance?"

Focusing Alison's attention on her favorite subject was the best way to distract her sister from pushing Jackie into dating more often.

After a half-hour of nonstop chatting, Jackie finally broke off the conversation so she could get some work done around the house. As she set the phone down, it rang again.

"What else could you possibly have left to tell me?" Jackie asked.

She was surprised when it wasn't Alison's voice, but rather Kris's that she heard. "Jackie?"

"Sorry, Kris. I thought it was my sister calling me back."

"The commander needs to see you. How soon can you get here?"

"What's it about?" Jackie asked.

"Can't say for sure. You don't seem to be in trouble, but he isn't happy for some reason."

"Okay. I'll be there within the hour." Jackie hung up the phone, then quickly changed into her uniform. *So much for my day off . . .*

So what is it?" Jackie asked as she entered the office. She indicated the closed door. "Who's in there now?"

"Captain Blakely. Still don't know. Something happened on alert last night and now shit's hit the fan," Kris said.

The door opened, and Tim Blakely came out grim-faced. "I'm sorry, Jackie. This really isn't fair to you." Blakely walked past, leaving Jackie to stare after him.

"Lieutenant Austin? Come in," Lieutenant Colonel Peter Reed call.

Lieutenant Colonel Reed was a tall, lean man in his early forties. As the squadron commander, Jackie had seen him often but never spent much time talking to him. He was well respected as an officer, but no one ever wanted to pull an alert with him—or any squadron commander for that matter. Squadron commanders had the reputation of sucking all the information out of a deputy's head like hyenas taking marrow from a bone. Then they would take all the best sleep shifts during the alert, leaving the deputy worn out the next day.

"Lieutenant Austin, relax. You're not in any trouble." Lieutenant Colonel Reed's attempt to put her at ease was unsuccessful.

Jackie took a seat across the desk from the solemn-faced officer.

"Let me start by making this official. I need to read you your rights." He read from a card, "You have the right to remain silent . . . "

Jackie sat in silent shock. What was happening? This didn't make sense! How could he say she was not in trouble one minute and then read her her rights the next?

When he finished reading, he looked up and asked, "Do you know Joel Perkins?"

Jackie hesitated. "Sure. He's in this squadron."

"I'm not going to ask how well you know him. I am going to ask if you've had an altercation with him recently."

"Well, a few months ago we had a run-in, but it wasn't anything serious." Jackie didn't know why she was trying to downplay the incident. Not sure where this was leading, she didn't want to reveal too much too soon.

"You'd better tell me about it—all of it. And let me start by saying that while I've already talked to other people in the squadron, I haven't talked to Lieutenant Perkins yet."

Jackie wondered if Kris was one of the people. Surely Kris would have warned her if she'd known what was going to happen.

~

Well that explains the anger," Lieutenant Colonel Reed said when he finished listening to Jackie's account. "Now we need to decide what we are going to do about it."

"Do? I don't want to do anything. I just want him to leave me alone."

"We've crossed that bridge. Captain Blakely came to see me this morning. Do you know what this is?" he asked, indicating the book in his hand.

"Looks like a log book."

"You mean a slam book?"

Jackie looked sheepish. Slam books were not permitted. They were hidden within the capsules where squadron commanders wouldn't find them. Usually they were full of stupid jokes, humiliating stories, or rantings about the chain of command. Jackie didn't bother even looking at them unless it was an especially boring alert.

Lieutenant Colonel Reed saved her further embarrassment by not waiting for an answer. "This slam book was recovered from Oscar capsule. There are some less-than-flattering things written about you in here. Did you know about that?"

Now Jackie was truly mortified. Not being certified for Oscar capsule, she had never pulled an alert there. She had no idea what was written in the slam book. "No, sir."

"It upset Captain Blakely enough that he felt it should be brought to my attention. Now I'm bringing it to yours. I'm going to give you some time alone to read it over. Then you and I need to take a walk." Lieutenant Colonel Reed handed Jackie the book and left, quietly closing the door behind him.

Jackie was shaking as she began to read where it had been bookmarked. At first, all that caught her eye was the many scribbled out parts, as if a name was being covered up. As Jackie read on she couldn't help but smile. It didn't take a rocket scientist to figure out that the scratched-out references were directed at the squadron commander. She was sure that hadn't escaped his attention either.

Then the smile quickly left her face as she reached the part referring to her.

"And that Jackie A thinks she's so hot. We all know she's sleeping her way to the top. I wonder how many times she had to go down on [scratched out section] to make the OA team. Wish she would 'spread' it around a little more. Haha."

Then the next marked page.

"That bitch Jackie is such a tease. I warn all you fellow missiliers out there, she is only looking after herself. She only wants to know what you can do for her. But if you can help her career, help yourself!"

Jackie dropped the book into her lap. She was so angry, hot tears stung her eyes. How many people had read this? Did anyone believe it? She read to the end of the book. After a short time, she wiped her face and walked to the door.

Lieutenant Colonel Reed was sitting next to Kris's desk. They both looked at her with grim expressions. Jackie asked quietly, "Where do we need to go?"

After what seemed to be an eternity, Lieutenant Colonel Reed came out of the base legal office and introduced Jackie to Major Dawn Suitor. Major Suitor shook her hand and indicated that Jackie should take a seat. Lieutenant Colonel Reed slipped out the door.

"Lieutenant Austin, as a staff judge advocate, I will tell you that we have enough evidence to charge Lieutenant Perkins with harassment and conduct unbecoming an officer. That's enough to have him discharged."

Jackie sat silently. This was so unreal to her. Things had all spun out of control.

Major Suitor continued. "But it won't be easy for you. If we go to court, you'll have to testify. Your name will be dragged through the mud. The defense will make you out to be the biggest slut on base."

Jackie looked up quickly, startled by the major's bluntness.

"I'm sorry to phrase it so harshly, but you'll have to get used to it.

"No."

"What?" the major asked.

"No. I don't want a trial. I don't care what happens to him. I want my life back."

Major Suitor was quiet for some time. "This is very serious. What happened to you should not happen to anyone."

Jackie thought, *You don't know the half of it.*

"Men shouldn't be able to get away with discrediting women because they're frustrated. But the fact is, they always get away with it to some degree. Even if they're punished, their victims become collateral damage," Major Suitor said.

"I will not let this vindictive asshole ruin my career. Men already have the choice whether or not to pull alerts with females. If it gets out that I made a complaint against Joel, no one will ever want to pull alert with me again. I'd be a leper."

"Obviously it's your choice, but you need to think long and hard about it."

Jackie stood. "Thank you, but I've made up my mind."

Chapter 26

Louis considered how to best approach Jackie. Her fear would cause her to reach out, and he wanted to be there for her. She wouldn't know who to trust, and he wanted her to know she could count on him to be the friend she needed now.

Louis knew how it felt to be the odd man out; as a military brat, he had spent a lot of time trying to fit in as they moved from one station to the next. He had attended three different high schools. It's hard to make friends on the move—he had made only two.

He felt his mind drift back to seventh grade, when he, Tom, and Drew were the Three Musketeers. Every weekend, they had a sleepover at one of the three houses. They built forts, entered go-cart races, and stayed up late. They were inseparable.

At the beginning of Easter vacation that year, Tom brought a pack of matches to the clubhouse. He had snatched them from his mother's purse. She probably had so many she would never miss them.

Tom showed the boys how to light a match, and they took turns striking the cardboard flint. When the pack was empty, the boys were disappointed. Tom promised to sneak some more for the next day.

Over the next few weeks, the boys pilfered matches wherever they could. They even walked to the corner market and shoplifted a few matchbooks. They didn't consider it truly stealing because the matches were giveaways to shoppers who bought cigarettes from the store.

Drew learned how to put a lighted match in his mouth without getting burned. Louis was fascinated to watch Drew close his lips around the lit match until nothing was left but smoke. Then he would blow smoke rings the way Louis had seen men do with cigars.

Louis didn't want to be outdone, so he started experimenting with fire even when the other boys weren't around. He wanted to impress them with his control of the flame. The fire was somehow comforting to him. He loved staring at the flame and watching it dance. Feeding the fire tiny pieces of paper or pencil shavings, he studied it to see if it would change colors.

Once he had mastered the art of fire-making, he taught Tom and Drew how to build a small campfire. They burned wood from the plethora of fallen trees in the nearby forest. The boys gathered rocks and bricks whenever they could to add them to their secret fire ring in the heart of the forest behind Drew's house. They cleared all the dead leaves away and raked the ground nearby to ensure no errant sparks would start a fire they couldn't control.

Toward the end of the summer, Louis brought something special to the campfire ring. As the boys went about building their fire, Louis thought about how pleased the others would be at the surprise. After the fire was burning at a good pace, Louis dug into his backpack and pulled out a squeeze bottle. He had seen his dad use this on the charcoal grill at home and the flames had shot high into the air.

"Watch this." Louis squirted the fluid into the fire.

"No!" yelled Tom when he saw what was happening, but it was too late. The flame raced back up the liquid and headed to the bottle in Louis's hands. Louis instinctively tossed the bottle away from him, but his aim couldn't have been worse.

As Drew turned toward the commotion, he was hit across the chest with a spray of flaming liquid.

Screaming, Drew beat at his chest with his hands. After a shocked hesitation, Tom rushed him, throwing him to the ground. The two boys rolled in the dirt as Louis stared in fascination. He had never seen fire travel like that. It seemed to jump through the air.

Finally, he snapped out of his reverie to hear Tom yelling for him to run for Drew's parents. Louis ran as he had never run before. The adrenaline pumped through his body, making his head swim. Leaves and branches slapped at his hands and face as he took the most direct route to the house. He remembered feeling the blows but not feeling any pain.

Drew's mother called the ambulance while his father ran into the woods. Louis was left standing in the kitchen, panting for breath. Although he was exhausted from the run, he had never felt more alive.

Drew was rushed to the hospital with second-degree burns on his hands and chest. Tom was declared a hero for his quick thinking. Louis was labeled an outcast.

Tom wasn't allowed to play with Louis anymore. When school started, the other kids gave him funny looks in the halls, whispering behind his back. Louis tried to ignore them, but it still hurt.

Soon after Drew was released from the hospital, Louis and his family moved again. Louis wasn't sure if this move was planned before the accident or if this was his parents' way of getting him away from the neighborhood gossip.

Either way had suited Louis just fine. This time he didn't go out of his way to make friends. He had other things to occupy his time, and he wasn't so sure he wanted to share them anyway.

At first, his parents watched him closely, hardly letting him out of their sight. Then their busy lives once again consumed all their attention, leaving Louis unsupervised. He could still pick up matches at a grocery store or gas stations, no problem there. He decided that making a fire pit in the woods was too tricky. There was always a chance someone would happen upon it, ruining his fun.

While exploring different routes on his way home from school one afternoon, Louis came across an abandoned building. He watched it for several days before venturing inside.

The building looked as though it had been a warehouse of some type. Aside from a few broken windows and lots of dust, it was in pretty good shape. Previous owners had left a broken table and a few rickety chairs. In one dark corner, he found the remains of an old kitchenette with a small burner, a sink, and cabinets.

Louis now had the ideal place to hone his craft. He gathered newspapers, scraps of wood, even plastic bits from the trash people left on the street. He scavenged anything that would burn.

Although Louis had learned his lesson about spraying lighter fluid directly onto fire, he expressed his artistic talent using flame on various mediums. Drawing lines on the cement with flammable fluids, he would then drop a match on them to watch the fire race from one end of the room to another.

The worst part about the warehouse were the cockroaches. Louis hated the black bugs that scampered in the shadows. To dispose of the despicable creatures, Louis sharpened a long stick and spent hours stabbing them, placing their wiggling bodies into the fire. They let off a slightly nasty smell, but the crackle as they burned was satisfying.

Louis's mind was brought back to the present when Jackie's front door opened. He slid down in the car seat, so his head wasn't visible above the steering wheel.

He had parked four houses down with a good view of Jackie's house. He knew she had alert today and would be leaving in time to get to the morning briefing. She seemed okay to Louis, but he knew better than anyone that a person could hide a secret. He had more than his fair share.

He would be there for her when she was ready.

Chapter 27

Officer Talley entered the squad room and made a beeline for Captain Shuster. "Cap, I think we have something."

Shuster looked up from his computer. "What is it?"

"Sedalia has had a recent homicide of a young, single woman. Warrensburg had one a few months ago. The MO is not the same. The only thing the cases have in common with ours is that all three were young women and there are no leads."

The modus operandi, or MO, was what most searches in the crime database were based on. A serial killer usually found one method of killing and stuck to it. Although escalation was not unusual, it was uncommon to kill using an assortment of weapons.

"It's a start. How did you figure this out?" Captain Shuster asked.

Talley ran his fingers through his hair. "Actually, my cousin was talking about the unsolved Sedalia murder at dinner last night. It got me thinking. I made a few calls when I got in this morning and came up with the Warrensburg murder."

"Good work. Did you get the files?"

"They're sending them over any minute. I'll let you know when I get them." Talley turned back to his desk, thinking that maybe they'd caught a break.

Chapter 28

The next few days, Jackie kept to herself, even avoiding the gym. She didn't want to accidentally run into Joel or any of his friends. Joel's stupidity was bound to cause major fallout.

As Jackie was drowning her sorrows in chocolate ice cream, she heard the front doorbell. She dropped her spoon into the carton and walked sluggishly to the front door. Kris was waiting impatiently for Jackie to open the lock. Jackie pushed the screen door open for her.

"How are you?" Kris asked as she hugged Jackie. "I've been worried about you."

"I'm okay. I'm not feeling social lately." She sighed.

"Well, I don't know if this is going to make things better or worse. Lieutenant Colonel Reed had Joel in the office today. He gave him an Article Fifteen."

"What? I told Lieutenant Colonel Reed I didn't want to press charges!" Jackie was livid. An Article Fifteen was the kiss of death for an officer. It was nonjudicial punishment under the Uniform Code of Military Justice, just a step below courts martial. Although considered a paperwork drill and not tried before the court, the decision was placed in a person's permanent record and was an issue when it came to promotion and assignment selection.

"This isn't just about you. Joel wrote some pretty nasty things in that book about the commander and several other people. Reed couldn't very well let it slide. Joel deserved to be punished." Kris looked intently at Jackie and added, "At least you won't be dragged through a trial. Joel accepted the Article Fifteen. He knows it could've been a lot worse."

"Now what's going to happen? Everyone's going to hate me."

"I doubt it. A lot of people have been talking about what he did, and they're pretty annoyed that Joel was so nasty. Not to mention, since he put a spotlight on all the slam books, the crews have pulled them from the capsules. I think they're more upset about losing their tradition."

"Come join me for ice cream," Jackie said as she headed to the kitchen. "I'll get another spoon."

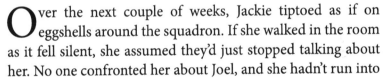

Over the next couple of weeks, Jackie tiptoed as if on eggshells around the squadron. If she walked in the room as it fell silent, she assumed they'd just stopped talking about her. No one confronted her about Joel, and she hadn't run into him at all since hearing about the Article Fifteen.

As Jackie walked to her car after finishing a late-night trainer, she noted to herself that she was finally starting to relax a bit. She'd done well that night, even receiving a compliment from the lead instructor. That's not easy when you work on the evaluation-side of the house.

Getting closer to her car, she noticed someone leaning up against it. She stiffened. Slowing her pace, she looked around to see if anyone else was within yelling distance. When the person straightened at her approach, Jackie prepared to bolt.

"Hey, Jackie, is that you?"

Jackie still wasn't sure who was talking to her, but the voice was familiar. She slowly advanced toward her car. When she got close enough, she recognized Ken Thompson, a crew commander in Delta Flight.

Jackie saluted. "Hi, Captain Thompson. Were you looking for me?"

He returned the salute casually and said, "I saw you getting ready to leave the squadron, and I wanted to talk." He hesitated, "I don't know if anyone else has told you, but no one blames you for that mess with Perkins. He's a jerk. Don't let it get to you."

A huge wave of relief washed over Jackie. "Thanks. I really needed to hear that."

"You're doing great. And remember, not all guys are like Perkins so don't put us all in the same basket." Thompson smiled. "I have to run. My daughter has softball practice." He waved as he walked to his car a few spaces down.

Jackie felt like celebrating. On a whim, she decided to see what Daniel was up to. Finding his car still in its spot at the hospital, she parked and went inside to track him down.

"So, what's a nice doc like you doing in a place like this?" Jackie teased as she leaned in the doorway to his office.

"Well, officially I'm not a doc so I don't have someone to do all this paperwork for me." Daniel's smile made her feel warm, and she felt her cheeks redden.

"To what do I owe this pleasure?" he asked.

"Oh, I didn't feel like going home yet so I thought I would see who else was avoiding an empty house."

"Who says I'm avoiding an empty house? Maybe I'm waiting for the party to heat up before I make my grand entrance," Daniel answered.

"And why wasn't I invited to your wild party?"

"Maybe I wanted to save you all for myself." Daniel smiled and leaned back in his chair.

~

Kris answered the playful knock that could only be Jackie. When she opened the door, Jackie gave her a quick hug, floating past her into the house.

"So, you're in an awfully good mood tonight. What happened?" Kris asked as she followed Jackie into the kitchen where Jackie was rummaging through the refrigerator looking for a cold drink.

"Things are looking up," Jackie answered with a smile, taking a long drink of the Diet Pepsi she'd found hidden behind leftovers.

"Is there someone helping your outlook?" Kris loved seeing Jackie in a better mood and was eager to share her excitement.

"I ran into Daniel at the hospital."

"Gee, I wonder how you happened to be at the hospital. I didn't realize the clinics were open this late."

Jackie threw a nearby dish towel at Kris, who caught it and smiled.

"So? Do I have to drag it out of you?" When Jackie didn't answer right away, Kris went on. "Does he make you feel dreamy? Are you falling in love?"

Jackie stared thoughtfully at nothing in particular. "No. Not love. It's nice to feel good for a change. To forget about work for a while, and Joel, and the effect he had on my career."

"How serious is Daniel?"

"I think it's too early to even be thinking like that at this point. I want a breather from guys crowding me—wanting something from me."

"And you don't think Daniel wants anything?"

Jackie paused, thinking about the implication. "I don't think he's in a hurry. He hasn't done more than kiss me goodnight. When I pull back, he doesn't pursue. That's a refreshing change."

❧

As Jackie called Daniel's number, she wondered if he was going to be irritated with her.

When the answering machine kicked on, Jackie said quickly, "Daniel, this is Jackie. I need to run to the office for a little while. I shouldn't be long. If you want to wait for me at my house, I'll be back as soon as possible. I left a key in the pipe by the cellar door."

Jackie wasn't sure Daniel would take her up on her offer to meet at the house. He didn't come over very often, and when he did, it was usually late and only to drop her off. But he was supposed to pick her up in half an hour, and she didn't think she would quite make it back in time. She wanted to be able to take off for their canoe trip as soon as she got back, so hoped he would be waiting for her. Kicking herself for forgetting to sign off on her technical order change yesterday, Jackie grabbed her jacket and ran out the front door, locking it behind her.

She returned home as quickly as she could. "Hey, are you here?" Jackie called as she opened the front door.

Daniel strolled in from the office at the back of the house. "What happened at work? Anything serious?"

"No. Just paperwork that I forgot to sign off on yesterday. Stupid mistake. I'm ready if you are." Jackie grabbed her backpack and slung it over one shoulder.

Daniel held the door as Jackie led the way.

❧

Do you and Daniel want to go out to dinner with us Friday night?" Kris asked Jackie when they had found a seat at their favorite tea room for lunch.

"I'll ask," Jackie answered hesitantly, "but he usually doesn't like to double date."

"I'm your best friend. Doesn't that rate?"

"Of course! He did come to your house once. That was a huge step for him. I practically had to drag him, but he had fun once we got there.

"I don't know what it is about him. He doesn't like going to any of the restaurants here in town, and he rarely comes to my house. Honestly, he'd be furious if he knew we were even talking about him."

"What do you mean? Girls talk about guys. Guys talk about girls. That's how it goes," Kris stated. "This can't be a surprise to a social worker."

"He's very private. He thinks our relationship should be between us. He doesn't even like me talking about him to my sister."

"Are you kidding?" Kris was incredulous. "Does he have any idea how close you two are?"

"I don't think so. He was an only child so the concept of growing up with a sibling is foreign to him. I guess he figures since we live so far apart that she isn't part of my life anymore."

"Well, did you set him straight?"

Jackie took a drink from the iced tea the waiter set in front of her. "No. He doesn't like talking about family. He changes the subject whenever I mention Alison . . . or you for that matter. He doesn't . . . " Jackie broke off.

"What? Doesn't understand relationships? Doesn't get the idea of social interaction? For goodness sake, he has studied the human psyche! What kind of counselor is he?" Kris was visibly annoyed now. The waiter placed their dishes before them and retreated. Kris mechanically bit into her chicken salad sandwich.

Jackie could see her friend was hurt and confused. She tried to think of a way to explain her relationship with Daniel to Kris. She felt as if she were digging herself into a hole. She knew the best way to get out was to stop digging, but she couldn't help herself. Feeling defensive, she needed Kris to understand.

"He likes it to be about us when we're together. No distractions. He doesn't talk about his past or family either." Jackie chose her next words carefully. "He's nice and treats me well."

Kris took another bite of her sandwich. Jackie could tell by the way she was purposefully chewing slowly that there was something else she wanted to say.

Chapter 29

When Jackie came back from alert, she stuck her head in Kris's office. Kris was on the phone but motioned for Jackie to wait. Jackie dropped her bags, taking a seat on the chair next to Kris's desk. She stole a curly fry from her lunch, and Kris slapped her hand away. Jackie snuck one more fry as Kris hung up the phone.

"How was your sleepover?" Kris asked with a grin.

"Oh, the usual. If it wasn't for all those annoying sirens, maintenance people, and constant phone calls, it would have been downright romantic." She didn't mind alerts. A routine job would've been too boring for her. "So what's been going on topside?"

"Alex's office had a work picnic yesterday. Shame you weren't there. You would've enjoyed it." The grin on Kris's face told Jackie there was more to this story. "But since you weren't there, I took the opportunity to do some exploring for you."

"Exploring . . ."

"What? Can't a friend make an innocent inquiry on her best friend's behalf?"

"What kind of inquiries and to whom?" Jackie laughed. Kris couldn't help it. She was a born matchmaker, and currently, her intended project was Jackie.

Kris tried to put on a straight face and act nonchalant. "Just a very nice young man I met. He's a friend of a friend at Alex's office. He was taking a break from the softball game, and we started chatting. Nice legs."

"You chatted about his legs?" Jackie questioned.

"No. That was an added bonus. He's tall, dark, and handsome. And he's single."

"Imagine that," Jackie said.

"I got his number—"

"I didn't know Alex was into threesomes."

Kris ignored her. "I thought maybe we could have him over some time and you could happen to stop by . . ."

"And 'happen' to be in my nicest outfit, fresh from the beauty parlor, I suppose."

"That's not a bad idea, now that you mention it," Kris said.

"We'll see." Jackie grabbed one more fry as she stood up. "I hear a hot shower calling my name. Catch you later." She waved as she left the room. *Kris is the best*, she thought with a smile.

After her shower, Jackie settled into her housekeeping chores. Although she dreaded the task, she knew it was time to catch up on her filing. She had bills, advertisements, and various letters piled on her desk that needed to be filed or shredded. Once she'd poured herself a glass of wine, she headed for the study. Staring at the mess on her desk, she thought, *Maybe I should've grabbed the bottle!*

She sat down, attacking the stack of papers off the top. Electric statements, gas statements, water statement . . . at least she wasn't behind on payments, just filing. *How long am I supposed to keep this stuff?* she wondered as she rolled over to the filing cabinet, opening the drawer. She noticed one file folder sticking up above the rest. Curious, she pulled it out. It was a file of old letters labeled "interesting reading."

Jackie loved rereading these when she was feeling down or lonely. She hadn't looked through the file since she moved in. She opened the folder, reaching for her glass of wine.

The cold chill ran down her spine. The letters were all upside down. That meant they were put in the folder backward. Jackie was compulsive and always filed her paperwork so that when you opened a folder, it read like a book. Quickly she glanced through her other folders, and they seemed to be filed correctly. What were the chances she would mess up only this one file?

She replaced the letters, arranging them to face the right direction. She was no longer in the mood to read. As she put the folder back in the drawer, she noticed the notepad sitting on top of the file cabinet.

The way the light was hitting it, Jackie saw the indentations left on the notebook from whatever was written on the last page that was used. She couldn't make out what it said, but the writing was large, and the indents were deep.

Curious to see if it would work like it did on TV, Jackie grabbed the notebook and a pencil. Using the side of the pencil, she lightly shaded over the page.

She was surprised to see a name and an address slowly appear as she colored down the page:

Neal Samson
213 Topover Ave
St Louis, MO

Jackie knew she hadn't written that address on this notebook. She hadn't talked to or thought about Neal in over a year. They had met at a conference and exchanged a few letters, but she certainly hadn't wanted another long-distance relationship.

Who could have written this and why? Then it dawned on her—Daniel. No one else had been in her house, besides

Kris, of course. Kris wouldn't care anything about Neal. Jackie opened the file drawer again, pulling out the old letters. Right on top was a letter from Neal, with his address at the bottom of the page.

Fuming, she replaced the file and started to pace. After circling the room a few times, she picked up the phone to call Kris. "Kris, this is Jackie."

"Hey, Jackie, what's up?"

"You will not believe what I found." Jackie recounted her discovery to Kris. "You didn't look through the letters, did you?"

"No. I didn't even know you had them," Kris answered. "But now that I do . . ."

"I can't believe it. It has to be Daniel. No one else has even been over. And I left him alone in my house! Why would he do this?" Jackie was irate and began kicking things.

"Calm down. I'll be right over. We'll figure this out. Maybe he had a good reason. Or maybe—"

Jackie cut her off, "Or maybe he's a sneaky, possessive creep!"

"Well, that is a possibility."

"You don't sound surprised."

"Let's say I wouldn't put it past him," Kris replied. "There is something about him . . ."

"And you're just now mentioning this to me? You didn't think I should know?" Jackie was incredulous.

"It was nothing I could put into words. It's just a weird feeling. It's the way he looks at you."

Jackie was silent. She didn't know how to respond.

"Besides, he was your counselor, right? Isn't that how you met? I asked a friend of mine who's a psychologist back home. She said he isn't supposed to date a patient."

"I'm not his patient," Jackie snapped.

"Not now, but you were. My friend says he could lose his license."

Jackie was silent as she considered that.

Kris went on. "I didn't want to mention it before. You seemed so happy. I didn't want to ruin it for you. But—"

"I gotta go," Jackie said abruptly.

"Jackie, don't be mad. Please. It was a feeling. I don't have anything concrete against him."

"I'll talk to you tomorrow." Jackie hung up the phone feeling betrayed, but she wasn't sure if the betrayer was Daniel or Kris.

Jackie was still frustrated when she awoke the next morning, so she called her sister. After filling her in on the details about the notebook and her conversation with Kris, Jackie took a deep breath.

"I think you're being too hard on Kris," Alison commented, as soon as she could get a word in.

Jackie thought about that. "But why can't Kris be happy for me? I finally found someone that I click with."

"Kris is thinking about what's best for you. You know she wants you to be happy, but she's picking up on things you're too close to notice."

Jackie sighed loudly. "This is infuriating. I feel like I'm only seeing select pieces of a huge puzzle that I'm expected to put together."

"That's the way life is. You'll never have all the pieces."

The girls were silent for a moment.

"Alison, remember when Dad used to bring his casework home with him and spread it across the kitchen table?"

"Sure. Mom would get mad because she didn't want us looking at it." The girls' father had been a police detective after he got out of the Army. Their mom used that as an excuse to explain his excessive drinking.

Jackie tried to act casual as she said, "I used to sneak in and look at the pictures. I wanted to see if I could figure out something Dad missed."

"That was no secret. I saw you in there poking around." Alison laughed. "Were you ever able to spot anything helpful?"

"Even if I had, Dad never would've listened to me. He always thought he knew more than everyone else."

"He was pretty good," Alison said. "And I think you inherited some of your reasoning skills from him."

"Really? I feel pretty helpless when my life is the mystery that needs solving."

"You're too close to this case. As Dad would say, it's hardest to sort through the weeds when you're sitting in the middle of them."

Jackie knew Alison was right but that didn't make it any less frustrating. She should be able to figure this out for herself.

"Think about it," Alison said. "You figured out Joel was writing the letters and tricked him into admitting it. You caught Daniel with the indentation on the paper thing. You don't give yourself enough credit."

Jackie smiled. Maybe she had picked up on some of her dad's better traits.

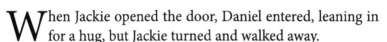

When Jackie opened the door, Daniel entered, leaning in for a hug, but Jackie turned and walked away.

Daniel closed the door behind him. "What's wrong with you?"

Jackie didn't say anything. She held up the notebook with Neal's address she had shaded.

At first, Daniel didn't respond. Then his face broke into a huge grin. "I knew you were smart."

Jackie couldn't believe her ears. "What?" she asked in disbelief.

Daniel tried to put his arms around her, but Jackie backed away.

"You're so smart. That's one of the things I love about you." Daniel seemed nonplussed about being found out.

"What are you doing going through my things?" Jackie stammered.

"I assumed when you gave me your key that it meant something. That you were ready to take things to the next level," Daniel answered without any trace of repentance.

Jackie couldn't believe her ears. "Next level? Does your idea of the next level mean spying on a person? Going through their personal belongings? Besides, I didn't give you a key. I left one for you for a one-time occasion."

"It's not spying when you're invited in," Daniel commented, totally ignoring her remark about the key. "It's sharing. I figured you wanted me to get to know you better. Isn't that why you invited me into your house when you weren't home? It was your way of opening up to me without having to say it."

Jackie stared at him.

"If I misinterpreted your intentions, I'm sorry." He reached into his pocket and took out his key ring. He removed her house key and handed it to her. Jackie hadn't even realized he still had it.

"I didn't mean to hurt your feelings." Daniel put his hands up, palms outward as a sign of surrender. "You can come into my house whenever you want and go through my things. It isn't a big deal. I have no secrets from you."

Jackie began to wonder if she was overreacting. She did want this to work out. They had so much in common.

She finally gave in, allowing him to hug her. His arms felt good around her, and she loved his woodsy smell. It gave her such a sense of peace, reminding her of camping in the backyard with her sister when she was little.

Jackie wondered if she had been blowing things out of proportion. Just because her dad could be a shit didn't mean that all guys were. Maybe she should give him a chance.

"Let's forget about it," she said. "But, please, don't go through my things. If you have a question, ask me. I won't hide things from you."

Daniel held her close for a long time.

Chapter 30

Hey, come on in. I didn't expect to see you," Kris said as she led the way into the kitchen. "Alex is working late tonight. He'll be sorry he missed you."

Kris's visitor replied with a shrug. "I'll catch up with him later. I was out this way and thought I'd stop by to see how the new garage was coming along. Sure looks good from the street."

Kris went into detail, explaining their progress and the plans for the next phase of building. "We have so much more to do on this house. I hope we have a chance to finish it before we leave. Do you want to see the garage?"

"Of course, lead the way."

Kris was completely absorbed in her description of the work still to be done. "Eventually we're going to put a stone path between the garage and the back door. That way we can avoid the mud when it rains."

She led the way into the garage. They'd made a lot of progress, but there were still tools on the workbench and piles of wood stacked haphazardly amidst the sawdust.

"So? What do you think?" Kris turned. Her smile turned into a look of confusion. He stood facing her with a hammer in his right hand. The head of the hammer rested in his left palm. Though the hammer caught her attention, it was his gloved left palm that raised an alarm.

"What—" Kris started.

In three quick strides, he was on her. The first blow glanced off the side of her head as she ducked, but it knocked her to the floor face down. She pushed herself to her knees, trying to crawl. She could see a thick board a few feet in front of her.

She felt the blow to her back, between the shoulder blades. Her face hit the ground again. She thought she heard something crack, but she wasn't sure of anything anymore. Nothing made sense.

She reached forward and touched the board. If only she could lift it and at least defend herself.

She saw a spray of blood. She wanted to scream but no sound would come. She was surprised it didn't hurt. In fact, she didn't feel much of anything.

As he rolled her over and looked into her eyes, all Kris could think was, *Who's going to clean this before Alex gets home?*

Chapter 31

Jackie got home and threw her bag into the bedroom. Noticing the light blinking on the answering machine, she pushed the button on her way to the kitchen. As she pulled out a soda, she heard Kris's recorded voice. "Hey, girl! Welcome home. Call me! I have some big news! Alex is working late so we get to have a girls' night until he gets back. I'll chill the wine!"

Jackie headed for the shower. Kris would have to wait a little longer to share her good news. Jackie needed to wash off the stink of the capsule.

An hour later, Jackie was headed through town toward Kris's house. She had tried to call but got no answer. Jackie figured Kris was sitting out back or had the music up too loud. From the sound of her voice, Jackie guessed she was in the mood to celebrate.

As she pulled up in front of the house, the lights were on and the front door was open.

"Hey, Kris! Where are you?" Jackie called as she walked through the front door. The stereo was playing, but it wasn't very loud.

She made her way into the kitchen but still saw no sign of Kris. *Maybe she's in the bathroom*, Jackie thought. She opened the refrigerator, pulling out the bottle of wine that was chilling. When Jackie had opened the bottle, poured two glasses, and changed the CD, Kris still hadn't emerged. Picking up the glasses, she headed to the master bedroom.

"Hey, if you guys are home and I'm interrupting something, let me know. Don't make me sit out here and wait!" When there was no answer, Jackie pushed the door open. The house was eerily quiet.

She walked past the bathroom, but it was empty.

Jackie went back to the kitchen. Taking another sip of her wine, she glanced out the back window. The lights were on in the garage. Little late to be doing construction. Jackie headed out the back door.

As she crossed the worn path in the yard, a strange smell caught her attention. Sweet, but not pleasantly so.

When she reached the opening that would someday house a door, Jackie dropped the wine glasses. She ran toward a figure on the floor but stopped a few feet away. The room started to spin. Jackie wanted it to stop because she couldn't think.

She looked wildly around the garage for an explanation. She spun around and raced out the door. She barely made it outside when she began to retch violently.

She made her way back to the house, struggling to hold herself together. Somehow she managed to find the phone and dial 911. The questions came at her so fast; she didn't have any answers. She dropped the phone and started vomiting again into the sink. Sinking to the floor, she lay there crying.

At some point, a blanket was wrapped around her shoulders. Strong arms lifted her, gently guiding Jackie to the couch. A glass of water was placed in her hands, and someone sat down next to her.

"Can you tell us what happened?" the voice asked.

Jackie looked up, but she wasn't focusing very well. Her eyes were swollen from crying, and she felt as though she'd been punched in the stomach.

"Start with your name," the woman prompted.

"Jackie. Jackie Austin," she croaked. Her voice sounded strange to her ears. This had to be a nightmare!

"Miss Austin, why were you here tonight?"

Jackie thought back to the phone message. Kris was so excited. She wanted to tell her something. "Kris called me. She wanted to celebrate something. She had wine in the fridge," Jackie's voice trailed off.

"Where is Kris's husband?" the officer asked. Jackie recognized the police uniform as she took in the woman speaking to her.

"He's working late. In Kansas City . . . "

"Kris!" A panicked male voice from the front porch pierced through Jackie's fog as Alex rushed through the door. Seeing Jackie on the couch wrapped in a blanket, Alex dropped to his knees beside her with concern. "Jackie, are you all right? Where's Kris?"

Jackie burst into tears again. She was sure her heart would break.

Alex's face contorted in pain. "No!" Alex wailed, jumping to his feet. He raced to their bedroom and flung open the door. "Kris!" When he came back to the living room and headed for the kitchen, a police officer stopped him.

"Sir. Sir!" the officer said more firmly. When Alex stopped trying to push past, the officer led him outside.

As Jackie watched him go, she noticed two pieces of paper on the floor under the kitchen table. Hoping they held some clue, she forced herself toward the table. The officer followed close behind.

Jackie bent down, picking up the papers. They were something from work.

"What is it?" the officer asked.

Jackie squinted at the pages. "They're assignment orders."

"What does that mean?"

She looked closely at the name printed on them, not believing her own eyes. "I'm going to Korea," she mumbled.

∽

Jackie moved through the house as if in a daze. She knew she should be doing something but couldn't make her mind focus on any task. Even the simple act of getting out of bed had turned into a chore.

The commander had removed her PRP status so she couldn't pull alerts. She wasn't even allowed to go to work. The Air Force couldn't permit someone in her questionable state of mind to be anywhere near nuclear weapons. She had no idea how long it would be. All they had told her was that she needed to take time off. When she was ready to come back to work, she would need to be reassessed before being PRP recertified to pull alerts.

As she wandered into the study, she saw the books of wallpaper samples lying on the floor. She and Kris had narrowed down the choices to two or three. Leaning over, Jackie picked up a book. It was so heavy.

Putting it on the desk, she flipped it open to the place they had bookmarked. The cheerful colors and fun patterns brought tears to her eyes. She reached down, fingering the page. Then, methodically and robotically, she began ripping page after page from the book, her movements becoming faster and more furious as she went. The tears flowed incessantly. She couldn't stop. When the book had been stripped clean, she hurled the empty cover at the wall.

"Why!" Jackie fell on her knees, raising her face to the ceiling. "What did she ever do to you?" she yelled at God.

She sprang to her feet and picked up the second book. Launching it across the room, she took out a lamp and end table. Spinning around, she swept everything off her desk, sending papers flying.

Finally exhausted, she sank into the chair, cradling her head in her arms, sobbing quietly. Eventually she drifted off into a troubled sleep.

~

The chaplain quietly closed the door and took his place in the circle.

"We're here because you were all friends with Kris. You shared memories and dreams with her," he said. "Kris will be missed, and her passing will cause pain. That's to be expected. It's normal and okay to hurt and to be angry."

He looked around the room, meeting as many eyes as he could. "But you have to understand that she's not hurting anymore. She's with God. She has never been happier." He paused to let this sink in. "Now we need to deal with your grief."

There was silence in the room, broken only by a few sniffles.

"Does anyone have anything they want to share about Kris?" The chaplain sat quietly, giving people time to gather their thoughts.

After a moment, Louis cleared his throat. "She was a great friend. I know people always say that about people after they're gone, but she really was. She listened when I needed to talk." His eyes drifted toward Jackie, then quickly returned to the floor. "She gave me good advice."

Jackie was reminded of how Kris had "advised" her at times. She smirked, then feeling guilty, covered her mouth with her hand.

"It's okay, Jackie," the chaplain said. "It's okay to have happy memories. Share your thought with us."

Jackie wasn't sure that the thought she was having was appropriate to share with a man of the cloth. Kris's advice to her usually centered around how to get a guy into bed. She quickly selected a safer story about when she and Kris had gone camping. She left out the part about the two bottles of wine they had consumed but shared the details about their midnight sprint into the river.

While the chuckles were dying down, the door opened and softly closed. Jackie looked up and was surprised to see Daniel enter the room. He murmured his apologies for being late and took a seat two people away from Jackie.

Someone else began to recount other stories of Kris, and Jackie felt a warm peace starting to settle over her. Jackie hadn't realized how many lives Kris had touched.

When Daniel starting speaking, Jackie was brought out of her reverie, and he had her full attention. It was so unlike him to share in a public setting.

"Kris's death was horrible. I didn't know her that well, so I didn't think it would hit me as hard as it has."

He paused, folding and unfolding his hands. "When I was eight years old, my sister was killed."

The silence was deafening. All eyes were on Daniel as he struggled to maintain his composure.

"She was nine. They still don't know all the details. They never found who did it."

Jackie was stunned. She didn't know Daniel had a sister. Why had he never told her?

"My parents had gone out for the night. We had a babysitter. I went to get Suzanne to play a game with me." Daniel choked back a sob. "When I went into her room, she was on the floor, and there was a lot of red. At first I thought she had spilled paint and that she was going to be in a lot of trouble," he paused before going on. "What a stupid thought."

He looked up, meeting Jackie's eyes. Seeing the tears in them, he tried to give her a reassuring smile.

"Jackie, I know how horrible this was for you. I wish there was something I could do to take the pain away."

Jackie couldn't hold back any longer. Bursting into tears, she ran from the room. She couldn't erase the pictures from her mind.

Chapter 32

The funeral was lovely. A lot of people from the base were there, including the squadron commander. Jackie didn't feel like speaking but stood near other missiliers, trying to absorb the strength to get through the service.

When Jackie approached Kris's mother in the receiving line, the older woman put her hand under Jackie's chin, lifting her face. "She loved you like a sister. I'm sorry you had to go through this."

Jackie burst into tears. Her daughter was dead, yet this woman felt sorry for Jackie. Jackie let herself be embraced. Their grief was so substantial that no words would be sufficient. She gave one final squeeze and moved away.

Alison took her arm, leading Jackie out of the church.

By the time they got to the parking lot, Jackie had regained her composure. She searched the parking lot for her car. In the front row, sitting on the hood of the car, smoking a cigarette was a familiar figure.

Jackie couldn't believe her eyes. She approached slowly at first but then broke into a run. As she got closer, he stood and spread his arms wide. Jackie reached him and buried her face in her father's chest. She felt her mother's presence behind her, gently stroking her hair.

~

The room was in total disarray, with boxes stacked everywhere. Jackie looked around for her soda among the mess.

"Hello?" she heard from the front of the house.

She weaved her way through the stacks into the living room to meet Daniel. He gave her a warm hug.

"What's going on?" He gestured to the dishes on the floor in the adjoining dining room.

Jackie hadn't spoken to Daniel much in the last few weeks. It was all too painful. Seeing him, she replayed her last conversation with Kris, remembering her misgivings about Jackie's relationship with Daniel. But, knowing what he'd been through with his sister, she felt a rush of guilt at having avoided him.

She wondered if others felt the same thing when they thought about Jackie. It was easier to avoid her than to think of the right thing to say.

"I got orders." There. She said it. It was real. She was leaving.

"What? Where?" Daniel was taken aback.

"Osan Air Base, Korea. It's a remote. Only one year."

"But why? Your friends are here."

"Kris isn't," Jackie answered, then instantly regretted her harsh tone.

Daniel sighed. "No, Kris isn't, but your network of support is here."

"I can't stay. It's time for me to go." Jackie started past him into the kitchen. "Do you want anything to drink?"

"Jackie, I want you to stop and think." He grabbed her arm, whirling her to face him. "How can you leave right now? Do you think Kris would want you to leave all your other friends behind at a time like this?"

"Kris was excited for me. She wanted to celebrate. She knew this was a great opportunity." Jackie paused before continuing. "I have to go. I have to get out of here."

Daniel was silent and fuming.

Jackie went on. "It's only one year. And to a fighter squadron. It'll be a nice change of pace to be around airplanes. We are in the Air Force, after all." She glanced at Daniel who was staring at the floor.

"What about this house? You put your life and soul into this house!" His voice was gaining in volume and intensity.

Jackie looked around. She felt a love for this house. This was where she had discovered her independence. It was more than a home. It was proof of her competence. She had demonstrated to herself and her father that she could stand on her own and make it.

She turned back to Daniel. "I do love this house, and it's been a great experience for me. I've learned a lot here. But in the end, it's a house. In a way, I've outgrown it. I need to move on." Jackie felt the words ring true as she said them. She really could walk away.

Daniel glared at her.

"I need you to understand. Kris was my best friend. There are so many memories tied to her here. Everything makes me think of her."

Daniel's face twisted with rage. He abruptly turned and stormed out the front door, slamming it behind him.

Hours later, Jackie opened the door, surprised to see Louis standing on her porch holding a bouquet of flowers.

"Hi. Come on in." She stepped back, holding the door for him.

"I heard you were leaving," Louis explained as he crossed the threshold, handing her the roses. "I wanted to make sure I had a chance to say good-bye."

"Thanks. That's so sweet of you. Would you like a drink or something?"

"Sure." Louis followed her into the kitchen. He watched as she pulled out a vase and started filling it with warm water. While it was filling, she opened the refrigerator. "Diet Pepsi or water?" she asked. "Or milk, of course."

"Diet Pepsi will be fine, thanks."

Jackie grabbed two sodas, handed him one, and went back to the sink. She shut off the water and pulled a pair of scissors from a top drawer in the cabinet. Efficiently she began trimming the ends off the stems and arranging the flowers in the vase. "These are beautiful."

"So are you," Louis answered.

Jackie looked at him.

"Sorry, I didn't mean to make you uncomfortable."

From the look in his eyes, Jackie wasn't sure he meant that. She got the feeling that was very much his intent.

"I appreciate the compliment anyway," Jackie said, trying to shrug off the eerie feeling. She finished with the flowers. "Let's go sit in the living room." She led the way to the front of the house.

"Are you excited about your assignment?" Louis asked as he took a seat on the couch.

Jackie settled herself into the armchair facing him. "Yes, I am actually. I wanted an overseas assignment. Europe was my first choice, but I was told that doing a one-year short tour is the best way to get there. The living conditions in Korea aren't the best, so it's hard to get people to volunteer. The assignment officer at the Air Force Personnel Center says that short tour returnees get first preference on assignments on their way out." She sipped her soda. "I hope they're telling the truth."

"I hope you get the follow-on assignment you're looking for. You deserve it after all this."

There was an empty silence.

Jackie asked, "What about you? How are you handling all this? We haven't really talked since I saw you at the chapel."

Louis shrugged. "I wasn't as close to Kris as you were. It's hard not seeing her at working group meetings on base." He hesitated. "I never knew anyone who died before . . . except my grandparents, of course, but that's not the same."

"I know what you mean. I hadn't either. I keep forgetting she's gone. I pick up the phone to call her, and then it hits me. I can't even bring myself to go into her neighborhood."

"Do you think it'll be better when they find who did this?"

Jackie thought about it. "In some ways. I won't be as scared to go outside, but it won't make me miss her any less."

"But you probably think moving to Korea is going to be safer for you."

Jackie gave an uneasy frown. "I wasn't thinking in terms of my safety. I was thinking more along the lines that a change of pace would help to occupy my mind."

"Well, I hope that works out for you."

"Me too. I'll miss the friends I've made, but the idea of starting over is inviting."

"We'll run into each other again," Louis predicted. "I'll have three years here at Whiteman about the time you leave Korea, so it'll be time for me to move. As they say, it's a small Air Force."

She smiled, thinking about how many times she had heard that saying.

"You should have let us give you a ceremony for pinning on captain," Louis said.

She shook her head. "It doesn't feel right celebrating anything right now. Besides, making captain is almost automatic, so it's not like it was a real accomplishment."

"But it's tradition," Louis said as he put down his empty can and stood. "Some things are worth doing."

Jackie rose with him.

Louis opened the door and then turned back to Jackie. Before she had a chance to react, he grabbed her in an embrace. As he hugged her close, he whispered, "We'll see each other again."

SECTION II

REPUBLIC OF KOREA, 1994

Chapter 33

Wow, fresh meat, was the first thought that went through Captain Stan "Mace" Mason's head when he looked up from the flight planning desk to see the trim brunette standing in the doorway with Lieutenant Colonel Mann. *And not bad either,* was his second thought.

The squadron commander escorted the young captain into the room, making introductions. "This is Jackie Austin, the new squadron section commander."

"So you're the new runner for the commander," a cocky young lieutenant commented.

The brunette smiled as she shook his hand without a word. Lieutenant Colonel Mann moved to the next officer in the room.

As Mace watched her interact with the other pilots—or more tellingly, the way they interacted with her—he made up his mind. When she and Lieutenant Colonel Mann were still three people away, he packed up what he was working on and slipped out the door. He imagined her eyes on him as he walked away.

∼

The next day was Friday and the end of a very long week. As Mace walked into the squadron to begin his preparation for that day's flight, he casually looked around for Captain Austin. *Oh, well,* he thought, *there's time.*

He strode to the briefing room to start his day.

After he'd finished briefing and put on his flying gear, he heard a captivating voice coming from near the operations desk. Mace and his flying partner, Captain Randy Gomez, headed in that direction.

"Sergeant Harris, do your thing," Captain Gomez said, indicating their readiness for the required "step" briefing. This briefing contained last-minute information the pilots needed to hear before they walked out to their planes—weather updates, flight line changes, and other pertinent reports.

Jackie finished her conversation with the young airman behind the counter and stood listening to the briefing. Mace could feel her eyes on him as he tried to pay attention to what the sergeant was saying. Everything was pretty standard, nothing new to worry about.

He signed off on the paperwork and turned around, but she was gone.

∽

*F*riday *nights in Korea are an event unto themselves.* Jackie watched the festivities in fascination.

Every fighter squadron had its own bar. Not simply a bar frequented by the fighter squadron members, but one actually in the squadron for the officers. Jackie wasn't sure if she was impressed by this or not.

The beer lamp was lit after the last sortie, or flight, for the day took off. There was always a tapped keg ready and harder stuff for those who didn't think beer was enough. This Friday was special because the newest squadron officers were being initiated into the squadron.

"So are you ready to get your coin?" the squadron section commander Jackie was replacing asked as they stood at the door of the squadron bar.

"I don't understand the whole coin thing," Jackie said.

"Each squadron designed their own coin. Once you earn your coin, you have to keep it on you at all times. And don't forget to get it engraved."

"Or what?"

The captain smiled. "If another officer coin checks you and you don't produce your coin, you'll be buying a lot of drinks."

Jackie laughed. "Figures it's all about drinking. What do I have to get on the engraving?"

"Today's date."

"Sounds simple enough." She gave him a dubious smile. "What do I have to do to get my coin?"

"Drink," he answered as he walked away.

Jackie watched as the guys hooted and hollered at the young lieutenants drinking their poison. The officers of the "Assym Dragons" were given a nasty concoction of various alcohols. It was served in the casing from a 35mm shell, standing six inches high and three inches in diameter, holding about four shots of alcohol at once.

While she sat trying to figure out how to avoid drinking her bullet, someone tapped her on the arm.

"Jackie, this is Mace Mason," said the section commander. "I'm taking off so he's going to make sure you get home. See you next week."

Jackie and Mace shook hands. Just as Jackie started to speak, Mace said, "I'll be over by the dartboard. Let me know when you're ready to go." With that, he turned and walked away. Jackie stared after him dumbfounded.

Guys had been chatting her up all day. She'd hardly gotten any work done because so many people wanted to meet the new girl. Mace didn't seem at all interested in her.

At that moment, the squadron commander took her arm, pulling her to her feet. Everyone started laughing when he handed her the ceremonial 35mm bullet reeking of strong liquor. Jackie turned to him and whispered, "Sir, I can't drink that much."

"Don't worry about it," he reassured her quietly so no one else could hear. "I mixed it myself, and it won't be that strong."

Jackie was relieved but still a bit embarrassed as everyone started chanting her name. She held her breath and put the bullet to her lips. As she started to chug she thought, *Here's to Korea!*

"A lison, you'll never believe how much they drink here!" Jackie explained to her sister in one of their rare phone conversations. Between the time difference and the expensive call rates, they'd had to cut back on their weekly chats.

Alison laughed. "I hope they're sober when they fly."

"I thought the same thing. Although they take their drinking seriously, they're even more unyielding about the twelve hours from bottle to throttle rule, meaning they can't drink any alcohol within twelve hours of getting in the plane. When they're preparing to fly, they're all business."

"That makes me feel a little better," Alison said.

In her short Air Force career, this was Jackie's first exposure to aircraft. Even though it was the only fighter she knew, she was convinced that the A-10 Warthog had the most exciting missions.

"The Warthog is known for being low and slow. The Army loves them," Jackie explained. "Their ability to fly so low allows them to get close enough to sort out good guys from bad guys in a close-in fight. They're great protection to the forces on the ground."

"You're really getting into this piloty stuff," Alison teased. "Tell me more about this new guy you wrote to me about. How can you fall for a guy who walks away from you?"

Jackie had written to her sister the Saturday morning after she had recovered from drinking her alcohol-filled bullet. She was sure the commander was telling the truth when he said he didn't make it strong, but it was still more than she was used to.

"Quite a tactic! I think it's working. I saw him again at the Officers' Club Friday night."

"What happened?"

"Practically the whole squadron was at the Officers' Club. I was standing in a circle of guys—literally! About eight single guys surrounded me, asking questions and making jokes. It was like a dream come true." Jackie laughed.

"Then Stan walked up to me. He said that if I wanted to get my coin engraved he would walk downtown with me. He told me where his dorm was and walked away. I didn't think much of it at the time because there were so many other people to talk to. Later though, I wondered where he had run off to. I don't remember seeing him again that night."

"So did you go?" Alison asked.

"Not on Saturday. I tried to find his dorm but couldn't. Honestly, I wasn't paying that much attention when he gave me directions, and this base is confusing. But the next night there was a going-away party for the group commander at the club. Which, by the way, is right across the parking lot from me. How convenient."

Alison laughed. "Try to come home with your liver intact, would you please?"

"So, the same group of guys were there—even more, because the other fighter squadron was also represented. They fly F-16s, so there's some bizarre, macho competition going on there. I saw Stan laughing with a group when I got there. I walked up to him and listened to him finish telling his story."

She paused to consider something. "Do you know, pilots talk with their hands more than any other group of people I know? And that's saying something because I couldn't speak if my hands were tied."

"No kidding! I think you get that from Dad."

"When he finished and the next pilot started telling his war story, I nudged Stan. I'm telling you, he has a gorgeous smile. I told him I looked for him and couldn't find his dorm, but that I really did want to go downtown. He drew me a map on a bar napkin, and we made plans to meet the next day. He left to get another beer, and I didn't see him the rest of the night."

"Are you sure there isn't something wrong with this guy? Seems a bit odd to me."

"I think it was a calculated plan. His strange behavior got me thinking more and more about him. I found myself wondering where he was and what he was up to. When we went to Songtan on Sunday, he was great. He was funny, polite, and easy to talk to. It was even comfortable when we weren't talking. There are a lot of lingerie stores downtown, so window shopping got a little awkward at times, but Stan kept making jokes; and not crude ones either. I found myself missing him when he wasn't around."

"Sounds serious," Alison said.

"Serious? I don't think so. If I couldn't meet a guy I wanted to marry in my whole time at Whiteman, I don't see it happening in one year in Korea."

"I guess you'll find out."

Chapter 34

Jackie is a breath of fresh air, Mace thought. On more than one occasion, he had seen her out on the flight line late at night—long after the majority of the squadron had left. She would walk between the A-10s, stopping to talk to the maintenance troops. He saw her laugh with them, and his heart flipped.

Her smile was wonderful, and her beauty was all-natural. She didn't seem pretentious or caught up in her appearance. After all, she wore the standard-issued Battle Dress Uniforms every day, and how flattering could they be?

The enlisted personnel seemed to appreciate her. Mace overheard the crew chiefs and maintainers make comments about the captain as they went about preparing their jets for flight. Some were the crude comments about her figure that one would expect, but more often than not, they expressed their surprise about how she treated them, how she really cared. Yes, she was doing well with the maintainers.

The pilots were a different story. An all-male population before she had arrived, they could come to work and be as naturally rude and crude as they wanted to be. And, since even most of the married men had left their wives stateside, they had let down their hair . . . what little they had.

With a woman on staff, Lieutenant Colonel Mann was trying to get the guys to clean up their acts a bit, and it wasn't going over well. It wasn't Jackie's fault. She could dish it out as well as she could take it.

Mace walked into the weapons office.

"Can you believe her nerve?!" Captain Jim "Zeke" Zechariah was spouting to whoever would listen.

"Now what?" Mace asked, grabbing a seat.

"I should call Social Actions," Zeke continued without pause. "See how she likes it."

"What's got your panties in a wad?"

Major Dan "Rolls" Rowling motioned Mace to follow him. They entered Jackie's empty office.

"So?" Mace asked.

Rolls walked to Jackie's locker in the corner, opening it to reveal pin-ups of guys with very little covering the parts that should be covered.

Mace and Rolls burst out laughing.

"What's so funny?"

The guys stopped, turning to the door in unison to see a composed Captain Austin leaning against the door jam.

Mace gestured toward the locker. "Friends of yours?"

"Only because they piss Zeke off." Jackie crossed the room and closed the locker. "He doesn't see the problem with hanging women's pictures in the weapons office, but apparently turn-about is not fair play. Lieutenant Colonel Mann already told me to take them down." She smiled. "Maybe I'll post them on Zeke's dorm room door."

Mace grinned back. Her smile was infectious.

She asked, "So, is there something I could help you with?"

Mace and Rolls shook their heads. Rolls said, "Keep up the good work with Zeke. He needs someone to bust his chops once in a while."

"And you're perfect for the job," Mace added.

As they left the office, Mace's hand brushed her arm. He felt a jolt of electricity and quickly glanced at her face.

She was blushing. He wondered if she had felt it too.

Jackie's first thought when she woke up was of Stan. She preferred to call him Stan because she wasn't a pilot and felt that call signs were a part of their silly club.

They were going to Inchon today. She couldn't wait to call Kris and tell her . . .

Jackie rolled over, putting the pillow over her head. She didn't bother fighting the tears that forced their way to the surface. The ache in her heart throbbed. There was so much she wanted to say. It crushed her that their last conversation had been a fight over Daniel. And Kris had been right. Daniel was selfish, and more than a little childish. He was angry that Jackie had an assignment. It wasn't as if she had a choice in the matter. When the Air Force said it was time to go, you went.

And Kris would be so thrilled about Stan.

Jackie allowed herself a few more tears before forcing herself out of bed. Stan would be by shortly, and she needed to get ready. She didn't want his impression of her to be that of a weak female.

Chapter 35

I really appreciate stopping by my house before we go." She fit the key in the lock, tossing her curls to one side and flirting over her shoulder. "I didn't plan on getting so dirty walking through the woods. I'll take a quick shower, and we can be on our way."

"No problem. I'm interested to see what your place looks like anyway." He followed as the young woman pushed open the door, dropping her purse on the kitchen counter.

She saw him take in the room quickly—white-washed cabinets, cheap Formica countertops, and linoleum flooring.

"Ignore the decor please," she said. "This house is in need of drastic remodeling. I can only do so much at a time though, so it's always a work in progress. Make yourself at home. I'll be right back."

"Take your time. I'll be here." He gave her a smile that made her knees weak.

She thought about how lucky she was as she headed to the bedroom. He was so wonderful. A little possessive perhaps, but it was nice to feel wanted.

He was the first man she'd gone out with since moving to Missouri, and it seemed to be going well. On their first date, he surprised her with flowers. She couldn't remember the last time a man had been so sweet.

She got undressed and adjusted the water temperature to the shower. While it warmed up, she began fantasizing about him. She left the door unlocked, half hoping that he would surprise her by joining her in the shower.

The thought excited her. She had to admit she didn't think it was likely. The few times he had kissed her, he'd seemed tentative, almost reserved. But those kisses . . . again she could feel the arousal and let herself enjoy it. She stepped into the shower, letting the warm water caress her skin.

The water turn on somewhere in the back bedroom. He'd completed his search of the kitchen and was going through the tables in the living room. He was very careful not to touch anything with his bare hands, using a towel from the kitchen to carefully open drawers and pick up items.

He moved into the bedroom, quickly and quietly searching the contents of the bedside stand. *And what do we have here?*

A box of condoms had been opened and at least a few were missing. His anger rose quickly, and a pressure was building in his head.

He heard the sound of the shower curtain being pulled back before he realized the water had been turned off, but he was rooted to the spot by the fury of discovering the condoms.

She stepped out of the bathroom wrapped in a towel, rubbing another towel over her wet hair. When she saw him standing beside the bed, she froze. He could tell when her eyes fell on the box of condoms in his hand. Then a smile spread over her face. She slowly dropped the towel she was using on her hair, taking a few steps toward him. Smiling in a way he was sure she thought was seductive, she reached up and tugged at the towel concealing her body, gingerly letting it fall to the floor.

He watched as she approached him. The sight of her sickened him. Why had he thought she would be any different from the rest? She was just a whore, like the others. She wasn't the innocent she pretended to be.

Before she took another step, he threw the box of condoms at her. Her face registered surprise and confusion. Too late, she stumbled toward the bathroom.

Quickly he closed the distance between them. He pinned her to the wall, holding her hands above her head. "You're a dirty whore," he hissed.

Despite his words, he felt himself growing hard, hating himself for it. He pressed his hips against her, and she too felt his erection.

Her fear was palpable as she started to scream. He released her long enough to use his fist to deliver a swift and efficient blow across her face.

He caught her as she slumped, laying her on the floor. His desire was overwhelming. He scanned the room wildly for the box of condoms he had thrown. It was under the bed. Still on his knees, he reached for it with one hand while he tugged at the zipper of his pants with the other.

Quickly he ripped open the package and pulled it out. When he reached down between his legs to slip the sleeve over his bulk, it had already dissipated. With his right hand, he massaged himself aggressively for a few moments, trying to revive what he had lost. When no reaction was forthcoming, his frustration reached its peak. He shoved his disappointment back into his pants, yanking his zipper back in place.

He got to his feet and paced the room. The young lady started to groan, moving slightly. In his anger, he grabbed the nearest thing—a table lamp. He heaved it at the woman, striking her full in the face and causing her nose to spray blood.

She cried out in pain. Striding purposefully to where it had landed, he picked it up, this time bringing it down solidly on her head, again and again. She fell silent and didn't move.

He sat back on his heels, catching his breath. After a few moments, he gathered her limp body in his arms, carrying her into the bathroom. He dropped her in the tub, and using a washcloth on the knob, turned the shower on to spray her body. He carefully washed the blood from his hands and face.

He went back into the bedroom. Grabbing a clean washcloth, he wiped down the lamp. He glanced around the room one last time. Picking up the box, foil wrapper, and condom he had attempted to use, he calmly walked out.

Chapter 36

Jackie pulled a chair closer with her feet, propping her boots on it. Stan sat in a third chair observing her profile. He liked how strong it was—plus this way he could watch her without her returning the stare.

The bar was quiet with the jukebox playing Queen in the background. Most of the guys from the squadron had taken the party to downtown Songtan where they would drink until half of them spent the night puking. Stan had stayed behind because he was engrossed in Jackie's story.

"Sorry I dumped on you like that," Jackie said self-consciously as she peeled the label from her beer bottle. "I guess a few beers sets me to talking."

"The shot of Jägermeister didn't hurt either," Stan added with a laugh. The nasty licorice-tasting liquor was a staple in a fighter squadron bar.

"That stuff tastes awful. How did you guys pick that to be a traditional drink in the squadron?"

"It's a fighter tradition. It doesn't have to make sense."

Jackie smiled and took a swig from her beer.

Stan turned the conversation back to Jackie's story. "I don't get why you didn't go to your squadron commander when all that crazy shit started happening."

"He didn't exactly seem the open and helpful type. During my 'welcome to the squadron' meeting, he told me that I better not even think about getting pregnant to avoid pulling alerts."

Stan choked on his beer. He wiped his mouth with the back of his sleeve. "Are you kidding me? He didn't really say that!"

Jackie nodded. "He also said that if I decided to go on the birth control pill, I had to report it to him immediately because I'd have to go DNIA for six weeks."

"DNIA?"

"Duties Not to Include Alert. I was one of the few women to pull alerts for the Minuteman Two missile. The doctors still weren't comfortable with how the pill would affect a woman when she first started taking it, so they didn't want her anywhere near nuclear weapons until they had a chance to observe her."

"And did the pill flip you out?"

"Wouldn't you like to know?" Jackie laughed. "Actually, the docs at Vandenberg warned us about that during training so I started taking it then—just in case. But I wasn't about to tell my commander."

"Well, after that kind of introduction, I can see why you were hesitant to talk to him." Stan continued to watch Jackie as she stared out the window into the dark.

Jackie set her beer on the table and stood up a little unsteadily. Stan jumped to his feet, balancing her with his hand on her elbow.

"I better get home," she managed to say.

"I'll walk you."

They didn't talk as they walked across the parking lot to Jackie's dorm. It was a warm night and the moon was shining full.

Jackie's room was the last one on the bottom floor. As she pulled her key out and fit it in the lock, she seemed nervous. When she turned to say good night, Stan was standing very close to her. She tilted her head to look into his eyes as he smiled a tender smile.

Placing a hand behind her head, he slowly drew her closer. Their mouths met, and he was on fire.

$\sim$

The insistent racket was unbearable. *Couldn't the Koreans wait until the afternoon to start their construction?* Jackie was having such a terrific dream.

The pounding continued.

She rolled over. *So, it wasn't a dream. He even smiles in his sleep,* she thought.

Now the pounding was accompanied by yelling. "Come on, Jackie! Open the door!"

Jackie jumped out of bed, wrapping a robe around her naked body. Adrenaline pumped through her as she tried to grasp why someone would be pounding at her door.

"What?" she practically yelled as she flung the door open.

Standing in front of her, still in his flight suit, was Randy Gomez. He had the decency to blush, and Jackie looked down to adjust her robe.

"What's so important? What time is it anyway?"

"Three in the morning. I need you to come get Zeke."

"Get him? From where? What happened?"

"He's being detained by security. He ran into a little trouble coming back on base."

Jackie sighed. "Wait while I get dressed. Then you can explain." Jackie closed the door on him.

When she went back to her room, Stan was leaning back on his elbows. "What's going on?"

"I need to bail Zeke out of jail. I'll fill you in when I get back," Jackie said as she pulled on her clothes.

"Do you want me to go with you?"

Jackie grinned. "No, thanks. Don't think I want to explain why I need a pilot to help me do my job." She leaned over, giving him a quick kiss.

Considering she was on her way to jail at three in the morning, Jackie was in an incredibly good mood. Maybe there would still be time for a second round if she finished up with Zeke quickly.

On the drive to the security police building, Gomez filled her in on what had happened. "We were on our way back from drinking downtown. When we walked through the gate to get back on base, Zeke started yelling that a car had swerved to hit him."

Jackie looked at Gomez in disbelief.

"Okay, so it was probably Zeke that swerved," Gomez admitted. "Then Zeke swung his bag of yaki and hit the car's trunk."

Jackie knew yaki mandu was pretty potent, but the small, deep-fried, meat-filled dumplings wouldn't do much damage to a car.

"The driver got out of the car and started yelling at Zeke. For some stupid reason—"

"Alcohol?" Jackie interjected.

"Yes, probably. Zeke took a swing at the man. His punch missed entirely, knocking him off balance, and he fell. A security policeman picked him up and escorted him to the detention cell. I convinced them not to call the squadron commander and promised to come get you instead."

As squadron section commander, Jackie had authority under the Uniform Code of Military Justice to administer punishment as required for certain offenses. It also meant she could deal with certain legal hassles so the squadron commander didn't have to be interrupted in the middle of the night and chance breaking his crew rest.

Crew rest was sacred for pilots. A pilot had to have at least eight hours of uninterrupted sleep when scheduled to fly the next day. The commander didn't get to fly as often as the others, so his flying time was sacrosanct. To interfere with that would guarantee a more severe punishment for the violator.

Jackie was only a captain and, as such, didn't administer punishment to other officers. Her job dealt mainly with the infractions of the enlisted men and women. But she could handle this part of the process.

She walked into the security forces building while Gomez waited in the car. After talking to the arresting officer and getting his side of the story, Jackie was able to convince him not to press charges, but she also had to promise that Zeke would go to counseling for his alcohol use.

She wasn't sure how the commander would handle the news tomorrow. An alcohol-related incident didn't look good on a person's record, but a pilot wasn't likely to agree easily to counseling. She signed the paperwork, promising to get Zeke home safely.

Jackie walked a very reticent Zeke to the car. Gomez and Jackie got Zeke settled in his room, then Gomez dropped Jackie back at her dorm.

"Thanks, Jackie. We owe you," Gomez said as she entered the building.

She waved, her thoughts already on something much more important.

Chapter 37

Twenty-fifth Fighter Squadron. This is Captain Austin. How may I help you?"

"Sure is good to hear your voice."

"Excuse me?"

"And the captain part sounds good too," said the familiar voice.

It took a few more seconds before Jackie placed the caller. "Louis?"

"Right on the first try. How are you, Jackie?" Louis sounded pleased with himself.

"I'm doing great! How are you? Where are you?" Jackie was curious how he had tracked her down. It wasn't that easy to place a call to Korea, especially with the time difference.

"I'm still at Whiteman although I should be getting orders soon. I'm trying for the east coast. Things are going okay. I miss seeing you around the base."

There was an awkward pause. Jackie broke it. "Have you heard anything—about Kris?"

"The police are no closer to an answer. They didn't have any leads to begin with. The newspapers gave it a lot of press for a while, but it tapered off. Now there are some rumblings about a serial killer."

"A what?!" Jackie was sure she had heard wrong.

"Right after you left there was another young woman found dead in her house in Knob Noster. The cops had no leads there either, but they started digging deeper and uncovered a few more unsolved murders within a couple hours' drive of here."

She took a deep breath.

"Jackie, are you okay?"

"I'll be fine. It's a shock. I can't believe anything that horrible could happen, especially around Warrensburg. And why Kris?" Jackie was near tears at the thought of her friend's last moments.

Louis was apologetic. "I didn't mean to upset you."

"It's okay. I asked."

"Well, now I feel horrible, and I still haven't told you why I really called."

"There's more?" Jackie suddenly felt very tired.

"I thought you should know," Louis hesitated.

"Go on."

"Joel is fighting his Article Fifteen. He's trying to get reinstated into the Air Force."

Shortly after the conflict with Jackie, the Air Force had a reduction in force in response to defense budget cuts. This happened on a cyclical basis and wasn't unusual. They usually started with anyone who had a blemish on their record and people who were eligible for retirement with over twenty years of service. Joel had been given his walking papers.

"You're kidding? That makes no sense." Jackie's head was reeling. "What possible grounds does he have to fight it?"

"I'm not sure. He has a civilian lawyer. I heard something about reverse discrimination. If it makes you feel any better, I don't think he stands a chance."

Jackie's thoughts were racing back to her conversation with the Air Force lawyer. "That means there might be a trial, doesn't it?"

"I suppose," Louis conceded, "but there are a lot of steps to go before then."

Louis tried to change the subject. "You should have your assignment by now, shouldn't you? I understand they make all assignments for people on one-year remote tours first. Where are you going?"

"Langley Air Force Base, Virginia. I'm going to be on the Air Combat Command staff."

"That's great! That's a big base and a pretty area. I have it on my dream sheet too," Louis commented.

"Louis, I've got to go. I don't mean to be short, but I have to get back to work." Jackie was still thinking about what would happen to her career if Joel's lawyer tried to drag her through the mud.

"Thanks for calling." She didn't even wait for a response as she hung up the receiver.

It was the second day of the exercise. Jackie was sweating as she walked to work in her MOPP-2 gear. She found a tour in Korea was unbelievably different than missiles. Here, every other month meant another version of military exercise to prepare them for war.

The MOPP level, or Mission Oriented Protective Posture, was designated by the threat in any given scenario. As the MOPP level number got lower, the more protective gear they had to put on.

In this exercise, the bad guys were already doing bombing runs. There were no signs of chemical weapons at this point, but the base leadership wasn't taking any chances.

Base personnel had to travel outdoors in MOPP-2, which meant that they were required to wear a charcoal-filled overgarment, rubber footwear covers, and protective helmet. Jackie had to be prepared to don her gas mask and gloves at the sound of the siren, warning that an attack was imminent.

Jackie went through the blast doors into the squadron and was met by one of her orderly room personnel checking ID cards. "Good morning, ma'am," he said.

"Good morning, Sergeant Williams. Anything exciting happening?"

"Not really. We've been diving under desks for every siren, but no exercise chemicals dropped yet."

"Guess that means it'll happen today," Jackie replied as she marched off in her rubber boots.

The usual contingent was gathered around the operations desk listening to the pilots getting ready to take off. Jackie dropped her bag on the desk and took her seat.

Her counterpart on the night shift was more than ready to let her take over. They quickly reviewed the change-over binder that highlighted anything important from the previous night. He gave her a mock salute, put on his helmet, and was off.

Jackie continued to read over the log from the night shift. She heard her name mentioned somewhere from the back room. She listened closely to try to make out the voices.

"I'll bet she would," someone said.

"No way. She has her sights set on Mace," someone else answered.

"Just watch. She's as fickle as all the others. Mace leaves in a few weeks. She knows he'll move on and forget about her. She has no chance at anything serious there."

Jackie pretended to be engrossed in the daily schedule when the two pilots entered the room and nudged each other.

Zeke said, "Hi, Jackie. What's up?"

Jackie looked up. "Hi, guys. Nothing much. Waiting for the next bomb to fall." She continued reading.

Gomez cleared his throat. "So, Jackie, are you going to the Christmas party?"

"I wasn't planning on it."

"Why not?" asked Zeke, trying to sound casual.

"Mace goes back to the states next week."

"Mace will find more than his share of chicks at his next base. There are still other guys in Korea who would take you to the party."

"Like who?"

"Zeke doesn't have a date," Gomez said.

Jackie looked from Gomez to Zeke. "Really?" She barely stopped herself from batting her eyelashes.

"Really," Gomez said quickly.

"Well." Jackie thought about it. "If you really wouldn't mind."

"What time do you want me to pick you up?" Zeke asked, a little too enthusiastically.

Jackie came around the desk. She got very close to Zeke, lowering her eyelids.

Zeke stepped back before he caught himself and stood his ground.

She stepped even closer, putting her hand on his chest. Zeke's heart was beating wildly. It was obvious to Jackie that Zeke was surprised by her touch.

She tilted her head and said just loudly enough for everyone in the operations room to hear, "When hell freezes over." She pushed past Zeke.

Zeke stood speechless while the other pilots in the nearby area burst into laughter.

SECTION III

VIRGINIA, 1995

Chapter 38

D aniel!"

"Surprise!" Daniel said as he wrapped Jackie in a hug.

Jackie hesitated a minute and then hugged him back. "What are you doing here?" she asked, gesturing to a seat in front of her desk.

"I just in-processed." Daniel took a seat. "I'm working in Mental Health for the First Fighter Wing. I heard you were here, so I had to track you down. You didn't tell me when you got your follow-on assignment."

"Korea was only a year, and it went by really quickly. We were constantly busy. It's so different in a flying squadron."

"What do you think of Langley? Where are you living? I'm meeting with a realtor later today to go house hunting," Daniel said.

"Knock, knock."

Both Daniel and Jackie turned toward the door.

"Hi, honey," Jackie said as Stan came into her office.

Daniel stood, so Jackie followed suit. "Stan, this is Daniel. Daniel, this is my husband, Stan."

Stan extended his hand.

Daniel gave a tight smile, gripping Stan's hand firmly. "Can't say I've heard much about you."

"Guess I'm too good for words."

"Not good enough for Jackie to change her name, I see," Daniel said.

"Stan would be an odd name for a girl, don't you think?" Stan responded, nonplussed.

He turned to Jackie. "Are you ready for lunch?" To Daniel he said, "You're welcome to join us."

"No, thanks," Daniel answered. "I've got things to do. Jackie, I'll see you around." He walked out of the office without another word.

Stan gave Jackie a questioning look. "Was that *the* Daniel?"

Jackie nodded, sighing. "And obviously he hadn't heard I was married."

"Cut him some slack. It wasn't like it was a long courtship or anything," Stan said.

"And whose fault was that?"

"I just couldn't live another day without you."

"Right," Jackie stretched out the word. "That and it was the only way to get stationed together."

"Isn't that what I said?"

Jackie grabbed her hat. "Let's eat."

~

It was great to hear Mae's voice. They hadn't talked much when Jackie was in Korea, but they had written often. Mae also had a place of honor with Jackie's family during the wedding.

"I loved the pictures you sent me of your new house," Mae told Jackie. "Your parents must be so pleased."

"Dad thinks I hit the jackpot with Stan. I think he was relieved to see someone finally married me."

"Oh, don't say that. Your dad is proud of you. I can tell by the way he looks at you. He was simply beaming at the wedding."

Jackie was pleased to hear that. Her dad had certainly mellowed over the years, but he had a long way to go before he would be warm. "That's what Mom said too."

"Your mom is a special lady. She certainly raised two lovely young ladies. How is Alison doing these days?"

"She's doing great. She has a new job working in advertising, so she can't get away as easily anymore, but it isn't too far for her to come on a long weekend. Only about a five-hour drive," Jackie explained.

"I'm glad. You two are so close."

"What about you? How are things in Warrensburg?"

"Quieting down. You know there were those awful stories about a serial killer in this area for a while but nothing else has happened for about six months, so the police think he's either stopped or relocated."

Jackie's stomach churned. "I hope he got hit by a bus and died painfully."

"I'm sorry, honey. I didn't mean to bring up tender memories. You know, the police never did connect Kris's death with the others. It didn't fit the pattern. The others were all single and living alone."

"It doesn't matter. He still deserves to die in agony."

"Jackie, let God deal in vengeance. The killer will get what's coming to him, and it'll be much worse than anything you can imagine."

"I know, I know. Let's change the topic. When are you coming to visit?"

"When do you want to see me?"

"Every day!" Jackie answered truthfully. "I miss you, Mae."

They made plans for a visit the following summer. Jackie was looking forward to showing Mae around Williamsburg.

Alison jumped out of the car and stretched. It should have been only five hours, but traffic had added another hour and a half.

Jackie came out the back door. "It's about time."

"Tell me about it! Next time, move closer, would you?"

"Talk to the Air Force." Jackie gave her sister a big hug. "Come in and see how I painted the guest room."

"You mean my room, don't you? Don't I get a say in the color?"

"Only if you want to paint it."

Alison followed Jackie through the kitchen, down the hall, and into the bright, airy guest room. The room was apart from the main living area of the house with a private bath.

"I like the green," Alison commented. "Now you need to get a new bedspread."

"Quit spending my money! I'll get to it eventually. Besides, if I wait long enough, Mom will buy it when she comes down. You know how she loves to shop." Alison and Jackie laughed.

"I've missed you. I wish you could stay longer," Jackie said.

"I miss you too, but I'm lucky I got this weekend."

"Are you hungry? Thirsty?"

"Thirsty. How about some wine? It was a long drive."

They went back into the kitchen, and Jackie pulled a bottle of German Riesling from the refrigerator. Alison rummaged through the cabinets until she found two wine glasses. "Where's Stan? Hiding from me?"

"He had to work late. He'll be home any time now."

They took their glasses out to the back deck. The large backyard ended in an acre of woods. The trees were so thick that the house behind them was completely hidden, even after the leaves had fallen.

"Is anyone going to build next door any time soon?" Alison asked, gesturing to the empty lot next to them.

"No. We met the owners. They're military but he has a few years before he retires, so they're going to hold off. It's mostly an investment, I think. The way land prices are going up around here, it should be worth quite a bit in a few years."

Jackie heard the doorbell ring inside the house. She set her glass down on the patio table. "I'll be right back. That's probably the package of books I've been waiting for."

When she came back out, Alison had her feet propped up on a patio chair. "Anything for me?"

"You can have this one." Jackie tossed a typed envelope without a return address on it to her. "It's probably one of my friends asking me to donate to their favorite charity."

Alison opened the envelope while Jackie sipped her wine, glancing through the books that had been delivered.

"Jackie?"

The anger in Alison's voice caused Jackie to look up in alarm. "What's wrong?"

"That son of a bitch!" Alison cursed. She got up, handing the letter to Jackie.

> *Ms. Austin,*
> *You haven't heard the end of this yet. I have a team of lawyers working on my case. Not only will I be reinstated in the Air Force, they will strip you of your rank, and you'll see how it feels to be on the street.*
> *You will get what is coming to you for your false accusations. Better get your affairs in order.*
> *- Joel Perkins*

"Can you believe the nerve of that guy?" Alison spouted after Jackie had a chance to read it. "How did he get your address?"

"A desperate man will stoop to desperate measures. It's probably not that hard to track down a person in the military.

We know a lot of the same people. Anyone could have told him where I was." She tossed the letter aside.

"Do you know where he lives now? Do you think he'll come here?"

Jackie tilted her head, thinking about it. "He was pretty pissed. I wouldn't put anything past him. Stan and I talked about this though. He says Joel doesn't have a case. Stan also assured me he would hire the best lawyers in the world to take care of me. I'm not going to let this asshole affect my life anymore. That would be giving him more power than he deserves."

"Where are my two favorite ladies?" Stan called from inside the house.

"We're out here waiting for you," Jackie yelled back. "Bring your own beer."

Stan came onto the deck with a beer in hand. Leaning over, he kissed Jackie and then gave Alison a hug when she stood to greet him.

"Good to see you, fly-boy," Alison said.

"Good to be seen. That means I'm still here. When did you get in?"

"Only a few minutes ago. I like what you've done with the yard."

Stan looked around. "There's a lot more to do. When those trees on the side grow in, they'll block any view from the future neighbors. The beds out front are almost done; I just need to put in the lights. It's dark out here at night, but it makes stargazing much more fun."

Alison glanced at the sunken hot tub. "I'll bet." She gave an exaggerated wink.

"Stan, let's go out for dinner," Jackie said.

"Let me change and finish my beer. You two pick the restaurant." Stan went back inside.

"He's great," Alison said.

"I know," Jackie agreed. "I guess my years of sorting through the not-quite-right finally paid off. Hey, speaking of not-quite-right, did I tell you Daniel is here?"

"You're kidding! When did he get here? Is he following you?"

"I don't think so. It's not that easy to finagle an assignment in the Air Force. I ran into him about a month ago. He said he was in-processing."

"That's freaky. Did Stan meet him yet?"

Jackie repeated their encounter in her office and was finishing up when Stan came back onto the deck.

"Move 'em out," he announced.

Chapter 39

I've missed this, he thought as he sat in his car watching the people go in and out of the store. "Too fat; too dark; not quite . . . ah, bingo," he mumbled quietly to himself.

Getting out of his car, he headed to the door at an easy pace. The brunette was ahead of him about thirty feet, working her way toward the hardware section. He smiled. *Just like old times.*

She stopped in front of the kitchen cabinets. He sidled up beside her and asked, "Oak or maple, do you think?" He gave her his winning smile.

She glanced at him and then back to the cabinets. "Oak."

"Are you redoing your kitchen?"

"No, I merely like to look at cabinets," she answered sarcastically, moving away to the other side of the display.

He was shocked. *Women don't talk to me this way.* He decided to walk away from this one and regroup. He was out of practice after all. Maybe he needed to use another approach.

He walked to the linens department where he saw a young woman looking at sheets. *Promising,* he thought.

As he walked down the aisle in her direction, a man approached from the other end, "How about this one?" the man asked, holding up a package.

Quickly the stalker stopped, feigning interest in a comforter. After what he felt was an appropriate amount of time, he turned, walking back the way he came. This had never happened to him before. It had always been so easy.

"Excuse me?" someone said. When he turned he saw a beautiful, young lady in her mid-twenties. "Would you mind helping me? I can't seem to reach that blanket on the top shelf." She smiled at him radiantly.

Now this was more like it. "I would be delighted to. He reached for the package she pointed out. Turning, he handed it to her. No wedding ring, he noticed.

"Here you are. Is there anything else I can help you with?" Again he flashed his grin.

"Thank you. No, I have everything else."

As he began to deliver his next line, she said, "This isn't too feminine, is it? My husband won't like it if it's too feminine." She was looking at the pattern on the blanket and missed the look of rage that flashed over his face.

When she looked up, he was gone.

Chapter 40

Stan handed Jackie a drink as he sat next to her on the picnic bench. It was a warm, late afternoon with just enough breeze to keep the bugs away. Perfect for Langley in the fall.

"So, where's this lieutenant you wanted me to meet?" Jackie asked.

Stan looked around with no results. "She'll be here eventually. She's probably still in the office."

"What's her story?"

"She reminds me a lot of you actually." Stan grinned. "She's a young lieutenant section commander in a squadron of fighter pilots. She's getting a lot of grief from the guys and taking it pretty hard. I thought you might have something in common."

Jackie shook her head. "When will you assholes learn that support officers are here to help you; not to put up with your shit?"

Defensively, he raised his hands. "It isn't me."

"But I don't suppose you told the guys to back off?" Jackie asked, already knowing the answer.

"Not yet. I want her to work through it if she can. If it gets too bad, I'll put a stop to it."

Jackie rolled her eyes.

"If I step in now, she'll lose the respect of the pilots. She can't afford that. They need to know she can hold her own," Stan explained.

"Right. I've heard that before."

"Here she is now." Stan stood to wave the young woman over.

Second Lieutenant Mary Wainwright was tall with auburn hair that brushed the top of her collar.

"Captain Mason, nice to see you," she said as she approached.

Stan signaled for her to join them. "We're not that formal around here. You should call me Mace. I want you to meet my wife, Jackie."

The ladies shook hands. "Nice to meet you, Captain Mason."

Jackie smiled. "It's Austin actually. I didn't change my name; no sense feeding the pilot ego more than necessary."

Grinning, Mary took a seat on the picnic bench across from the couple. "Life in a fighter squadron is a lot different than they tell you about in training."

Stan nodded to Jackie. "The stories she could tell . . . "

"Stan tells me you're from Ohio. What part?" Jackie asked.

"Wooster, near Cleveland," Mary answered.

"Well at least it isn't too far if you want to drive home for a visit. Nine hours, I think."

"Are you from Ohio too?"

Jackie nodded. "A little town about an hour south of Cleveland—Champion."

"Never heard of it."

Jackie chuckled. "I told you it was small. So how do you like Virginia? There are lots of things to do here."

"The location's great."

Jackie could tell from the look on Mary's face that something else was going on.

"What's up?"

Mary shrugged. "It isn't what I expected. People talk about the military becoming your family. These guys are far worse than my brothers, and they were a pain in the ass. Oh, sorry," Mary said sheepishly, glancing at Stan.

"It's no secret," he admitted freely.

"I agree with you," Jackie said. "Especially the young ones. They do grow up eventually, though it takes them longer than most men. I think it's the size of their toys."

"On that note, I'm going to get more drinks," Stan said, rising. "Can I get you ladies anything?"

"Beer," they replied in unison.

They watched Stan walk away. "Captain Mason isn't like that though," Mary said. "He's always nice to me and the enlisted folks in the squadron."

"Stan is older than the lieutenants. He had his time as an idiot, believe me. When I met him, he was a senior captain, but I heard the stories about him dropping his flight suit for a sock check in the squadron bar."

"What?" Mary couldn't believe it. "Captain Mason always seems so together." She hesitated before asking, "What's a sock check?"

"The guys in the squadron during pilot training were supposed to wear certain socks. I think it was a bonding thing, like wearing squadron t-shirts. If someone who outranked them called for a sock check, the guys would unzip their flight suits and drop them to the floor to reveal their socks."

"Wouldn't it have made more sense to lift their pant leg?"

"Definitely. But we are talking about pilots."

Both women enjoyed a good laugh.

Jackie got back on topic. "Don't let them get you down. Pilots will push your buttons to see you react. Don't give them the satisfaction and they'll stop eventually."

"Sounds like kindergarten," Mary muttered.

"It is in a way. For the lieutenants, they're just starting military school. Academies don't count because the atmosphere is so unreal to the rest of the world. You aren't a zoomie, are you?" Jackie asked, referencing the graduates from the United States Air Force Academy.

"No. I went through ROTC."

Jackie was also a product of the Reserve Officer Training Corps, so she could relate.

"The thing about ROTC is that you got to spend time in the real world, figure out how to pay your bills, and budget your time between drinking and studying. At the academy, all their thinking was done for them. Think of this as their freshman year in college."

"I see what you mean. My first year was rough. I was finally on my own with no one telling me I had to go to class. It was surprising I passed that year."

"It's not the same for everyone, but you get the idea. A lot of these fighter pilots are probably academy grads, and they've been told for the last four or more years how great they are. Getting picked up as fighter jock instead of tanker pilots reinforced it for them. They'll soon learn that there are pros and cons to every situation."

Mary gave a grim smile. "I wish they'd keep their stupidity confined to the workplace."

Jackie looked concerned. "What do you mean?"

Mary picked up a leaf from the table and started shredding it as she spoke. "I've been getting these annoying hang-ups in the middle of the night. No talking, just hang-ups."

A shudder ran down Jackie's spine. Her mind raced back to her time in Missouri. Time she was trying so hard to forget.

Stan and Jackie lay together in their king-sized bed listening to the birds outside the window.

"It's so peaceful out here," Jackie said. In the distance, they heard a car go by. There was very little traffic on their street of ten houses.

Stan rolled on his side, looping Jackie's long hair around his fingers. "So, what did Mary tell you?"

Jackie stared at the ceiling, thinking about her conversation with Mary. "It's hard to sort out. The stuff in the squadron is the petty crap to be expected."

"Did you tell her about your male pin-ups in the locker trick?"

"No, I have new material now. We worked up some plans to put an end to their foolishness. That stuff isn't bothering her all that much. It's the phone calls that are annoying her."

"Harassing calls? She can have those traced, right?"

"No, just hang-ups. She talked to the police and they told her she should change her number. She's already done that once, but it started up again. She's sure it's someone in the squadron."

"Why is she so certain?"

"Because the recall rosters have everyone's phone number on them, even the unlisted ones. How else would someone be getting a hold of her phone number?" Jackie explained.

"Good point." Stan thought for a minute. "What about someone else on base? It doesn't have to be someone in the squadron. That information is stored in plenty of places across the base."

"That's true, but who else would care enough to harass her?"

"Maybe someone she met at the club. Or in a meeting. It could be anyone. Someone she never even took notice of. You should know it doesn't take much."

She had shared with him what happened in Missouri, starting with the hang-ups and ending with Kris's death.

He had listened to her cry many times over the loss of her best friend. And every time he held her without the useless statement that everything would be all right.

Chapter 41

When Jackie arrived at six, the party at the Officers' Club was in full swing. The keg had been tapped, and the smell of burgers filled the air.

As Jackie made her way through the crowd she saw Mary sitting at one of the tables on the open patio. She changed course to say hello.

Once she got closer, Jackie noticed that Mary was sitting with someone.

"Hi, Jackie," Mary said when she caught sight of her. "Come join us. This is Daniel Evans. Daniel, this is Jackie."

Daniel didn't stand up but turned slightly, saying, "We've met."

"Oh," was all Mary managed.

Jackie grabbed the empty seat next to Mary, sitting down. "How are the burgers?"

"I'd recommend the sausages actually," Mary said.

Daniel stood, told Mary he would catch up with her later, and left to join another group of guys standing near the beer. Jackie watched him go and saw him down a beer in one long pull.

"What was that all about?" Mary asked.

"Daniel and I were stationed together at Whiteman. I must have offended him by getting married. How well do you know him?"

"Not that well. I met him about a week after he got here, a few months ago. He's called me a few times. He doesn't usually like to go out anywhere unless it's far from the base, and with my schedule, I don't have time for long drives."

Jackie shook her head in dismay. "He hasn't changed much. Watch out for him."

"What does that mean?"

"He gets possessive very quickly, and he has a temper."

"Thanks for the warning. I'll keep my distance." Mary shouldered Jackie playfully. "Let's go get you some food."

On their way to the food table, Jackie saw Louis arrive. She returned his wave, and he ambled over to them.

This is like old-home week, she thought cynically.

When he joined them, Jackie made introductions.

They shook hands politely.

Louis said, "I've seen you around. You hang with the guys from the Force Support Squadron. I've seen you at Anna's."

Mary raised her eyebrows. "You have a good memory. I'm sorry but I don't remember meeting you."

"You haven't. I don't hang with that group." Louis's straightforwardness made Mary a little uncomfortable.

"Where do you work?"

"At the hospital—in the admin section; I'm not a doc."

"I wanted hospital administration, but I got stuck as a section commander," Mary said.

"Hey, I resemble that remark," Jackie said. "What's wrong with being a section commander?"

"Nothing personal, Jackie. I've always wanted to work in a hospital but not in medicine. Things could be done so much more efficiently to improve patient care."

"I know exactly what you mean," Louis interjected. "I don't understand why hospitals enjoy taking advantage of the patient financially. It's like kicking a man when he's down." His face was animated with this topic.

Jackie saw the way Mary was looking at Louis and broke into a grin. "I think I need to go find Stan. I'll leave you two to get to know each other."

Jackie suspected they didn't even notice she had gone. When she glanced back they were deep in conversation about something. Jackie hoped Louis didn't start following Mary around like the puppy he had been in Missouri.

∿

Jackie picked up the phone on the second ring. "Jackie, I hate to ask this, but can you and Mace come over?"

"Mary, what's wrong?"

"I'm not sure, but something isn't right."

"We'll be right over."

They'd been to Mary's house several times over the past few months, but this time the drive was taking longer than Jackie remembered.

When Stan pulled up in front of the house twenty minutes later, all the lights were on as if a party was in full swing.

Jackie rang the doorbell and waited as Mary looked through the side window before unlocking the door for them.

"What's up?" Jackie asked, wrapping her arms around a very nervous Mary.

Stan closed the door behind them, following Mary into the living room.

As they sat down, Mary said, "It's probably nothing." Taking a deep breath, she went on. "I worked late tonight. When I got home, I noticed that the things on the porch were all rearranged. Stupid, huh? I probably would have passed it off as a prank, but some other odd things have been happening too."

"Like what?" Stan asked.

"Like my mail, for instance. I'll go a week with nothing at all in my mailbox. Then one day it'll be packed to overflowing. I talked to the mailman about it one Saturday, and he looked at me as if I were nuts. He said he doesn't remember delivering any unusually large amounts of mail to my address. And as for getting no mail at all, he said most houses get at least junk mail every day."

Jackie had goosebumps but didn't want to scare Mary more than she already was. "Are you still getting the hang-ups?"

Mary nodded. "Almost every night now. Usually I let them go to the answering machine. I don't feel like going through the hassle of having my number changed again."

"I think you need to call the police."

"They'll think I'm overreacting," Mary said. "I don't want to cry wolf. I thought maybe you two could help me think of alternate scenarios, other than the nightmares running through my brain."

Jackie knew exactly how she was feeling. But she also knew what could happen if Mary didn't take precautions. "Call them anyway. You don't know what kind of person is doing this. It's better not to take chances."

Stan stood up. "Have you checked the house already?"

"Briefly. I turned on all the lights and called you. The door was still locked and everything."

"I'm going to take a look around, if that's okay with you."

Mary looked relieved. "I'd appreciate it."

Stan walked toward the back of the house.

Jackie gave Mary's arms a reassuring squeeze. "You can stay with us."

"No, I don't want to impose. I'm being silly."

"Not at all," Jackie insisted. She had taken a real liking to Mary and felt the need to protect her. "I insist. Go pack some things."

Jackie saw the tears in her eyes. "Thanks. This means a lot to me."

"No problem. I'm sure you'd do the same for me."

Stan came back into the living room, reporting that everything was locked up tight. Mary excused herself to go into her bedroom.

Stan said, "You should get her to stay with us for a few nights."

Jackie stood, putting her arms around Stan. "I love you."

"You already asked her, didn't you?"

Jackie smiled, and Stan kissed her. "Great minds think alike," he said.

Chapter 42

The timing for Mary's visit worked out well because Stan had to go to Washington, D.C., for a conference and would be gone the whole week. Jackie was glad of the company.

One night after dinner, while walking around the property, Jackie told Mary about the house in Missouri and how much work she'd done to fix it up.

"It was a labor of love," Jackie explained. "Now I have another love to keep me busy. But I still like to keep a few projects going."

Jackie told her about tearing out the ceiling in her old house with a lead pipe and how she got stuck when she was trying to put the new sink in her bathroom. They laughed over the little mistakes Jackie had made and had to do over.

"But I wouldn't trade my time spent on that house for anything. It taught me so much about myself. I learned to stand on my own. And that I was strong enough to get through the rough spots." Jackie felt tears come to her eyes.

They talked long into the night. Jackie told her about how she met Stan and confessed she never planned on dating a pilot, let alone marry one. Eventually, Jackie told her a bit about Joel and the trouble he had caused her. She couldn't bring herself to mention Kris. She guessed Louis had probably already told her anyway.

"So what's happening with Louis?" Jackie asked.

"What do you mean?"

"You seemed to hit it off pretty well."

Mary smiled sheepishly. "He is kind of cute. We've gone out a few times."

"Good for you! You need to see the side of the Air Force that doesn't include rude pilots." Jackie was genuinely happy for her friend. She couldn't wait to tell Stan.

After the third night of sleeping in the guest room, Mary felt the need to get home and take back her life. Jackie supported her decision, although she was sorry to see her go. The police hadn't found any evidence of tampering around her house, and they were making regular drive-bys to watch for signs of trouble. So far, nothing was out of the ordinary.

After she left, Jackie wandered around the empty house feeling a bit lonely. It seemed strange to have the house all to herself. Stan wouldn't be home for another three days.

Flipping through the channels on the TV, she didn't find anything interesting. She shut off the television and thought about going for a walk, but noticed it was getting dark. She decided to do the dishes and turn in early.

As she ran the water in the sink, the lights flickered and went out.

"Damn." That was one bad thing about living so far out of town. The electricity was unstable at best. Rain or even high winds were enough to knock out power for a few hours. Jackie remained where she was for a few minutes, waiting to see if they would come back on. When they didn't, she shut off the tap, heading into the living room to get the flashlight they had for such an emergency.

She walked into the living room and caught a faint familiar odor she couldn't quite place. She paused as she tried to catch the smell again.

Sometimes her acute sense of smell was annoying, especially if it happened to be a particularly foul smell. She searched her memory to identify this scent. It wasn't triggering anything negative, but she lost the odor before she could put her finger on the memory.

Giving up, she bent down to grab the flashlight. Hearing a noise, she stood up to listen, holding her breath. When she didn't hear anything else, she chided herself for letting house noises scare her. Grabbing the flashlight, she turned back toward the kitchen.

Suddenly a hand covered her mouth, and an arm circled her waist, trapping one arm. She swung her free arm wildly in an attempt to connect with something vital. Her attacker was too quick for her, easily avoiding her blows.

Jackie kicked back with her right leg and connected with a shin bone. She tried to bite but tasted something rubbery. The hand slipped from her mouth to her throat. She felt the wind rush out of her as her attacker squeezed tightly around her middle. She continued to fight but felt the blackness coming on.

Then nothing.

Chapter 43

The house was lit up and people were talking nearby. Something was covering her nose and mouth, and Jackie panicked. She reached to pull the oxygen mask off but then heard Stan's voice.

"It's all right. I'm here." He took her hands, gazing into her eyes. He appeared to have been crying.

Stan said something to someone over his shoulder, then faced her again. "They said we can take this off as long as you're calm." He removed the mask from her face.

Jackie stayed very still. She wasn't sure if this was a nightmare or real. Stan wasn't supposed to be home for another three days. Where was Mary? She was confused.

"Mary?" she croaked out.

Stan looked down at her. "Her stuff isn't here. Did she go home? Do you want me to call her?"

Jackie tried to nod but her head was killing her.

The medic came over to check her eyes. "Your pupils are reacting fine, and nothing seems to be broken. Are you in pain?"

Jackie nodded again, wincing. Everything hurt.

"I'll give you something. It'll make you sleepy."

Stan said, "I'm going to call Mary's house. I'll be right back."

Jackie watched as the medic filled a syringe and stuck it into her arm.

Stan came back shortly. "Mary's fine. She's at home. I didn't tell her anything. I didn't want to spook her. She was glad she left before I got home. She didn't want to spoil our reunion."

Stan gave Jackie a wink and a smile. As always, he was making jokes.

Jackie was very thirsty. Stan must have read her mind. He helped her sit up and handed her a glass of water. As Jackie took it, she asked, "Why are you home?"

"I'm glad to see you too." He kissed her forehead. "We finished early, and I wanted to surprise you."

"Guess I wasn't the only one you surprised." The drugs were starting to take effect. The edge had gone from her headache, and she was feeling very tired.

"Did you see him?" Jackie asked.

"No, I'm sorry. He ran out the back. I was more concerned with you. You made a mess of our hardwood floor with the blood from that head wound."

Jackie felt the back of her head. A sharp pain went through to the front of her skull.

"The medic said head wounds bleed a lot. He put butterflies on the cut, and you don't need stitches."

Jackie looked around. Police officers were milling about the room looking at things. "This is like in the movies."

A policewoman approached them. "Do you mind if I ask you some questions?"

"Make it quick," Jackie said. "I feel the medicine kicking in."

Stan held her hand as she answered a litany of questions. All she knew for sure was that it was a man who was taller and much stronger than she was. He was able to lift her off the ground with one arm.

When she mentioned the taste of rubber, the policewoman explained that he was probably wearing latex gloves. That meant they weren't going to find any prints, but they'd look anyway.

"We'll need to take the clothes you're wearing to see if we can get any trace from them."

Jackie didn't object. Stan helped her off the gurney the medics had placed her on in preparation for transport if needed, and they walked into their bedroom. Gently he helped her remove her clothes.

His face tightened at the bruises that were already forming on her body. He slid her favorite nightshirt over her head, easing her onto the bed. Lying down on the pillow, she closed her eyes. She felt the sheet cover her but was too tired to say anything.

~

Mary hurried into Jackie's office talking a mile a minute, "Jackie, are you okay? Mace just told me. Why didn't you call? I would have come over."

Jackie smiled as she stood up. "Slow down. I'm fine."

Mary came around the desk and hugged her. "I can't believe it. If I had stayed a little longer, this wouldn't have happened."

Jackie hugged her back. "It isn't your fault. There's no way you could have known."

"What are you going to do? Do the police have any ideas?" Mary sank into a seat next to Jackie's desk.

Jackie sat back down. "They don't have anything to go on really. He was wearing gloves, and I didn't see anything."

"Did he say anything to you? What can you remember?"

Jackie searched her memory. She thought about the smell but dismissed it. "He didn't say anything."

"Why would anyone want to attack you?" Mary leaned forward on the edge of her chair.

"Not sure. It could have been a target of opportunity. Someone saw my lights on and found an open door." Jackie's mind wandered. It did seem like quite a coincidence. First Mary, then her. She was missing something.

Mary gasped. "Did I leave the door open?"

"No, that's not what I meant. Stop worrying. The police asked questions around the neighborhood. No one saw anything, but the houses are pretty far apart so that isn't surprising. Mace called an alarm company to install a system."

"What's the next step? What can we do to catch this guy?"

Jackie had been puzzling this very question over in her head. She wasn't sure what to do. The only thing she had was a smell that may or may not be connected. It was somehow familiar, but she couldn't describe it. Not much of a clue. She had an idea, but it wasn't fully formed yet. It was like going on a scavenger hunt using only her nose.

"My commander told me I need to talk to someone to make sure there are no lasting traumatic effects," Jackie answered.

"Hey, you can go see the base social worker! He's bound to help you."

Both girls laughed at their inside joke. Jackie doubted Daniel would be interested in helping her.

"Well, I'm glad you're okay." Mary stood. "I need to get back to work. Call me if you need anything. I mean it!"

She smiled as Mary slipped out the door.

Turning, Jackie stared out the window. Something was nagging at her.

Chapter 44

When the young lady got home from work, she dropped her bags on the kitchen counter and went to the refrigerator for a drink. Movement on the back porch caught her eye. Walking to the window, she saw a lone figure sitting on her porch swing. She slid open the patio door, and he turned to her.

"What are you doing here?" she asked him. They had only just recently met. For him to show up unannounced was quite presumptuous.

The man flashed a brilliant smile. "I wanted to surprise you."

Something in the way his eyes burned made her uncomfortable. "Well, you did that, but now you need to leave. I have company coming over."

She could see her lie reflected in his eyes. He wasn't going to let her off the hook that easily.

She was confused. They had hit it off when they talked in the park, but she certainly didn't expect this.

Pushing himself out of the swing, he stood. She took a step back toward the open door. He ran one hand through his hair and put the other hand on his hip. Flashing another smile, he said, "You said you weren't dating anyone. Who's coming over that's so important?"

She could see his face grow stony under the forced smile. Maybe she had embarrassed him. "It's not like that." She hesitated. "I guess I do have a little time. Let me get you something to drink. A beer?" Turning, she walked back into the kitchen.

As soon as she was safely inside, she slammed the sliding door closed and locked it. There was something not right about him, and she was scared. She ran to the front of the house, locking the front door.

She thought about calling the police, but what would she tell them? That some guy she had given her phone number to stopped by to surprise her? He hadn't done anything illegal—just creepy.

How did he even find her? She hadn't given him her last name or her address. Did he follow her?

When she returned to the kitchen, he was gone. Her flower pots had been knocked over, but she didn't see any other damage.

Chapter 45

I found the information you were looking for," Mae told Jackie over the phone. "But I don't understand why you want it. All that nasty murder stuff. It's stopped. That should be enough."

"Thanks for going to the newspaper office for me. Warrensburg is such a small town; I'm surprised they had anything on microfiche. I need to verify a few things."

Mae read her the information she'd requested as Jackie wrote it down.

When they had finished, Mae sighed, saying, "Honey, you need to let it go."

"I will, Mae, very soon," Jackie promised.

As soon as Jackie hung up the phone, she grabbed a footstool and carried it to her closet. Carefully she climbed the steps, pulling down a box she hadn't considered since she left Missouri. Blowing the dust off the top, she lifted the lid to reveal the contents. She dug past the old photo albums, pulling out the notes she had stored so long ago. Excitedly, she retreated down the steps and took her prize into her bedroom. Sitting cross-legged on the bed, she cracked open the journal and began to skim through the pages.

Cross-referencing the facts Mae gave her with the journal entries, she saw a pattern emerge. Jackie felt a weight lift from her shoulders that she'd been carrying since Kris's death.

❧

Jackie went in search of Louis at the base hospital. She ran into him outside his office.

"Jackie, what are you doing here?" Louis asked.

"I had an appointment, so I thought I'd say hi. She stepped closer to him.

He stepped back uncomfortably. "I'd love to chat, but I'm on my way to a meeting."

"No problem." She stepped closer again.

Louis stared at her inquisitively. "What's up with you? You're acting strange."

She waved her hand dismissively. "Lots of strange stuff going on lately, Louis. I'm going to get to the bottom of it."

"Do you need me to do something?"

"I think you've done enough," she said and walked away.

❧

He had a self-satisfied smile when he opened the door and saw Jackie standing there. "It's déjà vous," Daniel said.

She wasn't sure why she never noticed how irritating that look was before.

She gave a weak smile. "Yeah, it does seem like we've been here before."

"Does your husband know you're here to see me?" His voice dripped with contempt.

She shook her head. "Maybe this was a bad idea. I'll see if someone else can see me."

Daniel ran a hand over his face. "No, I'm sorry. That was very unprofessional of me. Let's start over. It should be easier for you to talk to me rather than someone else, not harder."

He gestured toward a chair. "Come in. Have a seat." He picked up a file, waving it in front of him. "I see your commander sent you over. As I recall, this is how we met in the first place."

Jackie took the seat closest to the door, easing herself down. She noticed the stale air in the room and glanced around, searching for the source. "Did he tell you why?" she asked.

"No details. All the referral says is 'traumatic event.' I think you're supposed to fill in the details." He settled into the seat behind his desk, tilting back in his chair.

She couldn't count how many times she'd seen him in that same position when they were dating. "It's no big deal really."

"Well, it had to be enough to get your boss concerned."

"Someone," she stopped, then began again. "Someone broke into my house."

Daniel sat forward in his chair. "Jackie, what happened?"

She stared straight ahead without focusing, trying to keep her composure. "I was home. Stan was out of town." Her voice broke at the memory. "The power went out. I went into the living room looking for a flashlight."

Daniel waited patiently for her to continue.

Taking a deep breath, she went on. "Someone grabbed me from behind. I tried to scream, but he put his hand over my mouth. He must have been wearing gloves. I can still taste the latex." Jackie shuddered.

Daniel came around the desk, kneeling beside Jackie. He took her hands in his. Again, that stale odor, but something else too. Jackie couldn't put her finger on it.

She lowered her eyes, trying to control her breathing.

"Were you hurt?" he asked gently.

"No. We struggled for a while. It's all a blur." A tear trickled down her cheek. "Then the next thing I knew, he let me go and ran away."

Daniel's thumbs made small circles on the back of her hands.

"Stan came home early. The man must have gotten scared and run away."

Daniel's hands stopped moving. Jackie looked up. He gave her hands a quick squeeze, letting them go. He stood up. Instead of going back to his chair, he leaned against the front of his desk.

"You must be the unluckiest person I know," Daniel said, stating the obvious. "First Missouri and now here. What are the chances?"

"I was thinking the same thing," Jackie replied. She sat quietly for a minute. "Did you know Louis is here at Langley?"

"He is? That's interesting . . . "

"I think he's the one that sent me the globe, and I saw him driving by my house at weird hours."

"Here?"

"No, in Missouri."

"And the letters?" Daniel prompted.

"Those were Joel. He practically admitted it."

"What about the phone calls?"

"Possibly. I don't know anymore!" She buried her face in her hands. "But I can't imagine either one of them would hate me enough to hurt me."

"Maybe the intruder didn't want to hurt you, just wanted to scare you. Could that be it?"

"No, I don't think so. I think I was fortunate. Stan came home early to surprise me and scared him off. He saved my life," Jackie finished with a whisper.

He grunted. "Seems to me that if he was really concerned he wouldn't have left you alone to begin with."

Jackie gave him a strange look. She wished he would get past this petty jealousy. "It's not as if we're attached at the hip. He has a job to do. He has to travel sometimes."

"You are married, aren't you? He should be there for you." He crossed his arms across his chest.

Jackie could hear the tension in his voice and tried to redirect the conversation. "Stan was there when I needed him. He scared the creep away."

Daniel sniffed, shaking his head. "If he'd truly wanted to hurt you, I think he could have done it."

"Maybe I hurt him when I was kicking. Or maybe he wasn't strong enough," Jackie suggested. "I was pretty scared. Maybe I'm overestimating his strength. That could be why he ran when Stan came in. He figured he could take a girl, but a man was too much for him."

Daniel pushed off from the desk and walked behind it. Sitting down in his chair facing her, he said, "You give your husband a lot of credit. I can't imagine anyone would be that intimidated by him, honestly."

"You don't know Stan very well."

"I know you made a mistake, and you're afraid to admit it."

"A mistake? Stan's the best thing that's ever happened to me."

Daniel shook his head, giving a sad laugh. "Jackie, as usual, you don't know what you're talking about."

Jackie looked at him in shocked amazement. "I'm not sure what this has to do with anything."

"You have issues you need to get past. That's why you're here."

"Are you saying the break-in was somehow my fault?"

He went on as if he hadn't heard her. "A relationship is more than a nice house and a roll in the hay. It's based on history and shared experiences. How long did you know this guy before you jumped in the sack with him?"

"That's none of your business." Jackie stood up. "This was a mistake. I shouldn't have come here."

Daniel stood, blocking her exit. "Maybe you should be asking yourself why you *did* come. Why to me?"

"I told you. My boss said I needed to talk to someone about what happened. He thought it would make me feel better."

Daniel stared at her, "But you could have gone to anyone. You chose me."

"My boss felt—" Jackie started.

"Again with your boss. Sounds like an excuse to see me again. You don't have to invent excuses. Just call. I could've tried to fit you in." Daniel's smug smile was unsettling.

Jackie didn't say anything.

"You came to me because you know you can count on me to be there for you. I'm here for you now like I was in Missouri. I've been with you through your toughest times—your scares in Missouri and Kris's death. You can't throw that aside like it doesn't mean anything. You can't just start over."

Jackie looked at him, not quite understanding. "I can, and I have."

"This is bigger than you. Try thinking about someone other than yourself." Daniel's words were coming faster now.

"When you walked through my door, things changed for me." He put his hands on her arms, gripping them gently. "Since I was little, I knew I was extraordinary. I knew I could have anything or anyone I wanted."

Daniel stared over her shoulder as if in a different place. "I see a woman; I decide; I act. There's never a doubt that I'll get the girl." He gave a regretful smile. "But they're always a disappointment." He shook himself from his musing and returned his focus to Jackie.

"You were different. I didn't pick you." He pointed his right index finger at her heart, slowly touched his chest, and said, "You picked me."

Chapter 46

Jackie didn't respond.

"It was a sign. Don't you see?" Daniel insisted. "Things were changing for me. It was time to take things in another direction."

"I came to you," Jackie insisted, "because my boss made me. There was nothing supernatural about it. The planets didn't align. It just happened."

The veins on the side of Daniel's neck bulged out. His face flushed and he took a few steps back.

She continued, "I was going through a lot during that time. It was a stressful situation—"

Daniel cut her off. "You don't get it, do you?"

"Get what?"

"You were special. You *are* special." Daniel emphasized. He was talking with his hands now.

"You walked right into my office." Daniel smiled broadly, "And you were feisty. You didn't even see me. You couldn't have cared less what I looked like or who I was. You had a single purpose, and you were focused. We're very much alike in that way."

Jackie watched Daniel, not sure what to say.

"It was refreshing. You were a challenge," he said.

His eyes as he smiled sent a chill down Jackie's spine.

"So I decided to see where it would lead," he said matter-of-factly. "You're the one."

Jackie's mouth went dry. She licked her lips, trying to stay calm. She had a million questions but the first one to her lips was, "The one for what?"

"For me, of course. You were meant to be mine. You were made for me."

"Daniel, I'm married."

Daniel continued as if he hadn't heard her. "We would've been together sooner if it wasn't for Kris. That was a little setback. Everything's coming together now."

"A setback?" Jackie was incredulous. "Kris was not a setback. She was my best friend."

"No, I was your best friend," Daniel snapped. "Kris got in the way. I was there for you even after Kris was gone."

"Kris was killed. She didn't leave me." Jackie tried to control the quaking of her voice. She was close to tears now.

"You're right. She didn't leave easily." Daniel was getting more and more agitated. "But in the end, she died, and I was there to pick up the pieces. That made it easier for us to be together."

Jackie held her breath.

"She had your orders, and she was happy about it. Happy! Can you believe it? She told me when I saw her at the club at lunch. She was so excited for you. She had no thought for my plans. Does that make sense if she was your friend? I'm the one who would make you happy."

"Daniel, Kris didn't make the assignment. She was the messenger."

He rubbed his eyes wearily, ignoring her. "After she died, I thought for sure you would turn down your assignment and stay with me. I could have arranged for a hardship, what with your friend being killed and all. The leadership would have understood."

Daniel began to pace in the small office. "You were convinced somehow to go to Korea. But I waited. I'm a patient man." He wasn't even looking at Jackie. He was talking more to himself than to her.

"Daniel, did you hurt Kris?" Jackie was afraid of the answer but needed to hear it.

"If I did, why would I tell you?"

"Sorry, it was a stupid question."

"It's the wrong question," Daniel insisted.

"What's the right question?"

"What wouldn't I do for you? For us?"

Her heart beat wildly as she tried to keep a calm outward appearance. She changed tactics. "I know you could never do anything to hurt someone. You don't have it in you."

"What does that mean?" Daniel asked sharply.

Jackie walked back to her chair, turning her back on Daniel. She sat down, gesturing dismissively. "Nothing. It isn't important."

Standing in front of her, he looked down at Jackie. "What?"

"It's just that you don't seem, well, you know—"

"I don't know," Daniel snapped.

"Well, you aren't that physically aggressive. Sure, you talk a big game, but think about it. We went out for how long in Missouri? And you never even made a move on me. I figured I wasn't your," she wavered, ". . . type."

Chapter 47

The unspoken accusation hung in the air.

Daniel's face grew beet red. "I was being respectful to what we would become. If you only knew what I was capable of," he said in a low voice. "You wouldn't dismiss me so easily."

"Oh, Kris told me I should give up on you. That you wouldn't change. You probably leaned the other way. I wanted to give you a chance, but she said you were too soft to be a real man."

Daniel slammed his hand down on the desk causing Jackie to jump.

"Soft?" he spat out. "Guess I changed her mind about that one, didn't I? Too bad it was too late for her to share her new opinion of me with you!"

Her stomach turned. She couldn't believe she let herself get so close to this guy. What kind of a monster was he?

"You can be sure none of the others thought I was soft. I'm not one to cross, Jackie. They learned that the hard way. I thought you were different. Maybe you need to be taught a lesson too."

She could feel the sweat running between her breasts as her heart pumped madly. She got up quickly, but Daniel was by her side before she could reach the door.

He pinned her body to the wall with his own, his hands holding her arms. His face was inches from hers, and she could smell the stale beer on his breath.

Jackie looked into his wild, blue eyes.

With an unwavering gaze, she began a low, soft chuckle. In a husky voice, she said, "Kris was all wrong about you. You aren't soft at all."

Daniel relaxed his grip slightly on her arms, taking a half step back to get a better look at her face. When he saw her sly smile, he gradually broke into a grin.

Jackie continued in a silky voice. "She didn't appreciate you. I'll bet she didn't even expect you to swing the hammer. Even at the last moment, she didn't believe it, did she?" Jackie raised her right hand to stroke his cheek, smiling continuously.

"She had no idea," Daniel confirmed.

He pressed his body against hers, and she felt his hardness pushing into her side.

"The look of shock on her face was even better than the others," he said.

Jackie slowly raised both arms, locking her hands behind Daniel's neck, lovingly gazing into his eyes.

"Others?" she whispered, leaning forward to nibble on his earlobe seductively.

Daniel closed his eyes at her touch. He cleared his throat. "Of course she wasn't the first, but she was the easiest." He began to grind against her now.

Jackie pushed him away to look into his eyes again. With a look of awe and excitement, she stated, "It was you! Those other women!"

He grinned like a small boy receiving praise from his mother. "But that's all over. Now that I have you, I don't need anyone else," he assured her.

After a pause, she added, "And Mary?"

"Wainwright?" Daniel clarified. "Sure, I made a few calls. I figured it worked for you; it might work again. Maybe she would come see me—professionally, of course."

"So you were the one making those calls to me in Missouri?" Jackie asked quietly.

"Not at first," Daniel said with a quiet laugh. "It was probably that idiot Joel. It was his style. But it did spook you a bit, and I kind of liked that. I kept it going after he gave up on you."

Daniel gently stroked her cheek as he spoke. "I told you I will never give up."

"Kris had no idea what you were capable of."

Daniel continued to bask in the praise. "As long as you understand me. That's all that matters." He leaned forward to kiss her.

She put her index finger on his lips. "Yes, Daniel, I see everything you're capable of."

Jackie summoned up all her strength, driving her right knee into Daniel's groin as hard as she could.

As he doubled over in pain, Jackie quickly sidestepped, grabbing the back of his head and driving it into the wall she had been leaning against. He slumped to the floor.

At the sound of the crash, the door to the office flew open. Agents from the Air Force Office of Special Investigations poured in.

They pulled Daniel to his feet. He watched in disbelief as Jackie reached under her uniform blouse, ripping off the wires taped there. She handed them to the agent standing outside the door.

Stan was waiting anxiously for her. He looked into Jackie's eyes intently, as if trying to determine if she were okay. She smiled weakly back at him. He laid a hand on her upper arm, then walked past her into the office.

While the agents were busy handcuffing Daniel and reading him his rights, Stan took the opportunity to get close to Daniel, who was obviously confused by the whole scene.

Stan's right fist connected soundly against Daniel's left jaw, knocking him to the ground again.

One agent grabbed for Daniel while the other one shoved Stan hard in the chest, pushing him toward the door.

Stan walked back to Jackie, enfolding her in his arms. She buried her face in his chest as the agents hauled Daniel from the building.

Epilogue

Stan held Jackie in his arms as they swayed together on the deck swing. The air was cool and crisp. The birds twittered overhead. Alison was sitting in a nearby wicker chair.

"So, you finally talked to the base chaplain?" Alison asked quietly, not wanting to break the mood.

A small smile crossed Jackie's lips. "I did."

"And? Do you feel better?" Stan asked.

Jackie nestled closer into Stan's arms. "I do. My boss ordered me to talk to someone, but he didn't say I had to go to Mental Health. I figured it was time I gave God another chance. Doing it on my own wasn't working."

"Wait a minute . . . did Chaplain Vandesteeg help you hatch this plot to catch that psycho?" Alison asked.

"We did it together. Chaplain Vandensteeg knew I had to take the steps that would finally nail that bastard."

"What made you suspect Daniel though?"

Jackie thought for a moment. "It was too much of a coincidence that he was here and at Whiteman, and the hang-ups happened at both places."

"But so was Louis. Or who knows where that Joel character is. Or it could have been someone you didn't know you knew—if that makes sense," Alison said.

"Louis is a little over the top when it comes to attention, but I don't see it in him," Jackie said.

She went on. "I thought about Joel, but he was pretty forthright in his anger. He was a jerk, and he never tried to hide that. I don't think he would sneak around. Plus, he had no connection to Mary. I also checked with some mutual friends. He couldn't have been in Virginia the night I was attacked. He received a job in California and was moving in that weekend."

"Daniel was a creep. I could see that the first time I met him," Stan said.

"To be fair, you were prejudiced by the stories I had told you. Daniel has a mean streak that he kept pretty well hidden at first," Jackie said. "He was attentive, considerate, and charming, but when things didn't go his way, his veneer began to crack a bit."

"So why follow you here?" Alison wanted to know.

"Apparently he never let go. When he got here and realized I was married, he must have decided to try to re-enact how we met with someone else. He saw Mary on base somewhere and tracked down her phone number. He probably figured if she got stressed like I did, her boss would send her to him as mine did. Working in the hospital, it wouldn't have taken much to get her phone number, even after she changed it."

"I told you Mary was a lot like you," Stan said. "Apparently Daniel thought so too."

They all sat quietly for a minute, thinking about all that had happened.

Jackie broke the silence, "The clincher was the smell. Remember? There was a familiar odor before I was attacked. It took me the longest time to place it. I ruled out Louis first. He still wears the same cologne he wore in Missouri. But when Daniel got near me, I was sure. It was his soap, such a distinctive smell."

"What about the other murders? How did you know about those?" Alison asked.

"To be honest, that was only a feeling. I had no proof. I was convinced that he was involved with Kris's death, but I didn't know enough about the other women to make the connection. I did get a funny feeling when Mae mentioned the killings had stopped. Seemed like too much of a coincidence. I did some digging and crosschecked dates. I know Joel was on alert for some of those murders. Although I don't know where Daniel was, I can tell you he wasn't with me. He always had mysterious 'friends' he had to see or appointments he had to keep. I thought it was related to his work, so I never questioned it. I'd jotted down a few of those dates in my journal in passing; it must have seemed important to me then. They matched two of the murders. I guess I should have probed more at the time."

"There was no reason for you to suspect him then," Alison replied. "Whose idea was it to wire you?"

"Chaplain Vandesteeg took me to the OSI after we talked, and the agent agreed to try it. The agent thought it was a long shot at best. I can't blame him."

"I want it on record that I was very much against the idea of using you for bait," Stan said protectively.

Jackie squeezed his arm. "I know. But I needed to do this. I needed to make him stop."

Alison smiled. "I'm glad you decided to give God another chance."

"Talk with the chaplain," Stan paused for dramatic effect, "and come up with the idea to catch a killer." He shook his head in disbelief. "That's quite a leap."

"Sometimes faith is taking that leap," Jackie smiled at Alison.

Alison grinned back proudly. "Jackie gets her intuition from Dad. They're both good at unearthing the truth. It comes natural to them. I think Jackie must have inherited my share too," Alison commented.

Jackie continued her explanation. "Daniel was trying to play God himself. He was trying to decide who would fall in love with him and when. He wanted things when he wanted them. He would decide who to forgive and who to punish. He acted as if the world was there for him."

"Sounds pretty conceited to me," Stan said.

"He was definitely that. Environment played a role in who he became, but he still had the final say. Becoming a social worker put him in the perfect position to use his talent for helping or hurting. He made the wrong choice. He used his talents to manipulate and control others instead of healing them."

"There are other people who have grown up in worse situations than Daniel. What made him a killer?" Alison asked.

"Daniel took it to an extreme. His temper tantrums had been perfected at an early age—hence his ability to get whatever he wanted from his parents. I hear they're even going to look into the death of his sister again. Maybe it wasn't an accident. Maybe it was his first murderous rage."

"And the guilt his parents felt over the death of his sister caused them to give in to him even more." Stan was catching on.

"Exactly. He was rewarded for killing his sister by getting everything he ever wanted. As he got older, the tantrums didn't work as well, but his looks and charm took him far," Jackie said.

"But that doesn't explain why he didn't kill you," Stan stated the obvious, which neither one of them had wanted to address before. "I know you're really special and all that," he gave her a playful squeeze, "but you certainly aren't the type to give in easily to a spoiled brat. How were you different?"

"I'm not sure. I think I was lucky. I must've given him the attention he needed at the time, so he thought we had something special."

"Kris knew something was off about him," Alison said.

"I feel horrible that she may have been killed because of me," Jackie said.

"Daniel is the only one to blame here. Not you," Stan said.

"And Kris didn't realize how right she was," Alison said.

Stan hugged Jackie. "I'm sure she knows now."

#########

A Note from the Author

Many of the interactions in the book are taken from true-life stories that I lived as a missile launch officer. The murders were thankfully not true, although the lessons gained as "Jackie" moved through the Air Force were sincere.

I spent twelve years on active duty with the U.S. Air Force and met my husband at Osan Air Base in Korea. With the impending birth of our second child, I transitioned to the Air Force Reserve and completed close to twenty-eight years of service.

I retired as a colonel out of the Pentagon after working for the Secretary of the Air Force and have many more interesting stories to share about Air Force life. I enjoy fiction writing and incorporating true stories from a female officer's point of view.

Being one of the first female launch officers on a co-ed crew for the Minuteman II introduced me to situations that women following in my footsteps hopefully won't have to bear. Just as the first women at the military academies broke new ground and opened doors, so will the women who break into newly opened career fields.

We are the greatest Air Force in the world, but even we suffer growing pains. Women have a lot to contribute, and I think the Air Force gives them the chance to spread their wings (pun intended).

I truly believe that the Air Force is ahead of society in its acceptance of change, while still holding all to high standards.

Follow Jackie to Spangdahlem Air Base, Germany in *Wind the Clock,* then come to D.C. with her in *Truth Has No Agenda.* Her life doesn't slow down much.

Excerpt from Wind the Clock

He started to shiver violently from the cold. He couldn't get up. Someone would see him.

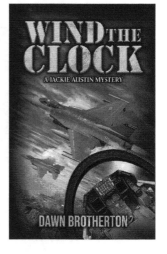

"Over here!" someone shouted.

Finally, he thought. A light flashed across his face, turning the inside of his eyelids red. He kept his eyes closed, but he couldn't control the shudders that racked his body.

"Hurry. Call the ambulance." Someone rushed off and the mutterings of a phone call reached his ear.

"Hang in there." Now the voice was directed at him. He felt relief as something warm and heavy was draped over his chest.

"He has cuts all over his body, and his leg is at a funny angle." This was a new voice. "He's shaking a lot."

There was a long pause and then, "Hey, Major, should he be shaking like this?"

Major Jackie Austin rushed to the prone man and quickly assessed his condition.

"Damn it, Bobby! Get off the ground!" Major Austin grabbed him by the arm and yanked the injured man to his feet. "Somebody get the ambulance here!"

"You idiot!" She picked up the jacket that had fallen to the ground and wrapped it around him.

Bobby was confused. Why was she mad at him? He played his part well.

The fake blood the exercise team applied a few hours ago covered most of his face, but his lips were blue, and that was real.

"You're supposed to be my medical expert. How can you evaluate the responders if you go into hypothermic shock?" She rubbed his shoulders violently, trying to get his blood flowing.

Bobby heard the sirens and willed them to move faster. He had made a stupid, stupid mistake. Within the next few minutes, the ambulance screeched to a stop only yards away.

"We got it, Major." The medic moved her gently aside. Jackie took a last look at Bobby, turned away, and stomped off, swearing at herself. She kicked a stone, and it rattled off in the darkness.

"Now what do you want us to do?" someone asked.

Bobby looked around at the medics checking his vitals. They had piled heavy blankets on him, and his shivering was quieting finally. He wanted to know how his mistake was going to affect the rest of the exercise.

Major Austin turned back to the waiting men, taking charge. "Read from the script. Give the responders the results they would have received from Staff Sergeant Ford and let them call it in." The young lieutenant rushed back to the waiting crowd and began to take control of the chaos that had quickly erupted.

Bobby watched as Major Austin dropped her head and shook it silently for a few minutes before walking to the ambulance. As they loaded him into the back, she leaned into the open doors. "You okay, Bobby?"

"Yes, ma'am," he replied from under the mounds of blankets. "I'm sorry."

"No, it was my fault. I should have known better. I didn't realize it would take them so long to find you. I should've planned better."

"You can't plan the weather," he said with a weak smile. Although early September in Germany was fairly mild, the nights got chilly. The day had started out beautiful, but with no cloud cover to trap the heat, the temperature dropped quickly when the sun went down.

She patted his booted foot. "I'll be over to the hospital in a few minutes. Do me a favor and evaluate how they treat you, okay?"

"Yes, ma'am. That'll ensure I get the royal treatment," he said between chattering teeth.

Jackie stepped back, and the medic closed the doors. Immediately the ambulance pulled away with its lights flashing. No sirens though. Bobby assumed that was a good sign.

About the Author

Colonel (retired) DAWN BROTHERTON is an award-winning author and featured speaker. When it comes to exceptional writing, Dawn draws on her experience as a retired colonel from the U.S. Air Force as well as a softball coach, Girl Scout leader, and quilter. Her books include the Jackie Austin Mysteries, cozy mystery *Eastover Treasures*, YA Fantasy *The Dragons of Silent Mountain*, and romance *Untimely Love*.

She has also completed four books (*Trish's Team; Margie Makes a Difference; Nicole's New Friend,* and *Tammy Tries Baseball*) in the middle grade Lady Tigers series, encouraging female athletes to reach for the stars in the game they love.

With the help of former Disney illustrator Chad Thompson, Dawn has released her first children's picture book (ages 3-7) *If I Look Like You* and its accompanying activity book, *Scout and Her Friends.* These books help children explore STEM and non-STEM career fields as they learn they do not have to change who they are to fit in.

Under nonfiction, the *Baseball/Softball Scorebook* was created with instructions written for those not as familiar with the intricacies of the game.

In other nonfiction, *The Road to Publishing* is designed to walk writers through the maze of becoming a published author, whether self-publishing, traditional-publishing, or somewhere in between.

Dawn is a contributing author to the non-fiction *A-10s over Kosovo,* sharing stories from her deployment, and *Water from Wellspring,* a collection of short stories about how God has worked in people's lives.

For more information about Dawn's books and book signings, go to www.DawnBrothertonAuthor.com.